2032

2032

STEPHEN COMER

LUMINARE PRESS
WWW.LUMINAREPRESS.COM

2032
Copyright © 2024 by Stephen Comer

All rights reserved. This book or any portion thereof may not be reproduced or used in any manner whatsoever without the express written permission of the publisher, except for the use of brief quotations in a book review.

Printed in the United States of America

Luminare Press
442 Charnelton St.
Eugene, OR 97401
www.luminarepress.com

LCCN: 2024904318
ISBN: 979-8-88679-513-4

To Asimov, Heinlein and all the other great science fiction authors who made my childhood a world of wonder and optimism, my profound thanks.

Contents

Chapter One: Qubits a Dollar 1

Chapter Two: The Senator 17

Chapter Three: The Agency is Summoned 33

Chapter Four: The Chase Begins 55

Chapter Five: Montana 71

Chapter Six: Expansion 91

Chapter Seven: It Gets Darker Before the Light 101

Chapter Eight: The Task Force 107

Chapter Nine: The Briefing 131

Chapter Ten: The Interrogation 147

Chapter Eleven: A Plan Unfolds 175

Chapter Twelve: Dar-Ki 185

Chapter Thirteen: Epilogue 205

About the Author 211

CHAPTER ONE

QUBITS A DOLLAR

Monday, April 5, 2029—5:45 PM PDST

It was a bright cold day in April.

A tall, gangly twelve year old walks across his bedroom to dim the lights. The room is not exactly what you would expect a typical teenage boy's room to be. The clutter is not comprised of Star Wars action figures, dog-eared automobile magazines and model cars, but is instead a cornucopia of physics textbooks and random pieces of homemade beaker stands, bunsen burners, test tubes and other paraphanalia one would normally expect to find in a fairly well-equipped high school science class.

Bill, the boy's best friend is standing on the opposite side of the room as the teenager clicks off the bedroom light. Outside the drawn curtained windows a storm is brewing. The occasional lightning flashes and accompanying claps of thunder add to the air of tension and anticipation of what is to come.

The boy bends down behind the small table he has sat up in the middle of the room. On the table he has erected the most powerful laser pointer he could find in a holding stand. In front of the laser pointer he has mounted a sheet of overhead transparency film on which he has carefully and meticulously copied a half-centimeter defraction grating pattern which he downloaded from the internet. In the center of the pattern is a fork-shaped pattern which, if he has copied it with sufficient clarity, should defract the coherent laser beam into a series of circles onto the wall against which Bill is standing. He has explained to Bill that as he centers the beam onto the fork that Bill will see a dark circle magically appear in the center of the concentrated beam, giving evidence that the coherent beam of light is being "twisted," thus proving the principle of angular momentum predicted by the strange and magical theories of quantum mechanics.

As he moves the laser pointer slowly and meticulously onto the fork in the middle of the defraction grid, a brilliant flash of lightning fills the room with blinding white light. The laser beam surges with an accompanying roar that sounds like a guitar amp cranked to maximum power. The thin red laser light turns sun bright in a millisecond, burning a pencil thick black hole straight through Bill's forehead before he collapses to the floor.

Dr. Charles Westwood's head bolts upright off the workbench on which he has fallen asleep, awaking from his now-familiar nightmare. He is sweating profusely and he swears under his breath as he looks around at his small, cluttered shed in a sleepy town on the outskirts of Silicon

Valley where he has toiled away tirelessly on his life's greatest obsession: Quantum computing.

For years, he has been consumed by the idea of inventing the world's first successful quantum computer. While the world at large was still captivated by classical computers, Charles was among those computer researchers who believed that quantum computing held the key to unlocking the mysteries of the universe.

Charles' journey began in his childhood. His parents were both brilliant scientists, and their home was filled with books, gadgets, and endless discussions about the wonders of science. From a young age, he was fascinated by the potential of computers. But as he delved deeper into the field, he became frustrated with the limitations of ordinary binary computers. "There has to be a better way than counting zeros and ones," he would sometimes say out loud to himself.

As he grew older, Charles focused his studies on physics and was particularly fascinated with the weirdly fascinating world of quantum mechanics. He voraciously consumed books, attended lectures, and spent countless hours conducting experiments like the quantum cryptography experiment with sunglasses, or the particle detector experiment using a foil tray and alcohol, or the laser pointer angular momentum experiment which, unlike his nightmare, had correctly proven the theory when he demonstrated it for his friend, Bill. His obsession with quantum computing was born out of a dream: A dream of a machine that could solve complex problems in seconds, a dream of a device that could simulate the behavior of molecules and atoms with unparalleled precision, and a dream of a future where humanity could finally unravel the mysteries of the universe.

It was higher education that had proven to be Charles' salvation. High school had seemed more like an endurance contest. He had little interest in socialization. Bill had been the closest thing to a best friend. The two would hang out together, going roller skating, biking and, most importantly, conducting their science experiments in Charles' bedroom and having long discussions about the mysteries of science. High school itself was just boring. Charles found that his science teachers knew less about his favorite subject than he so often viewed him as a nuisance which they merely tolerated.

But higher education had been totally different. He attended UC Berkley as an undergraduate in part because of its academic reputation but also because it was nearby which allowed him to continue to expand his personal lab. His parents had kindly allowed him to construct a small shop in the corner of their backyard. In it he had transferred all the paraphanalia from his bedroom. At Berkley he found like-minded lab instructors who were more than willing to give him outdated or damaged equipment from the school's physics laboratories to add to his collection. But these material additions were nothing compared to the creative minds with which he found himself surrounded. He spent every spare moment in the labs joyfully completing his class assignments while engaging in challenging debates around his passionate hopes for the application of quantum physics to computers.

After graduating with honors from Berkley he was awarded a full scholarship to enroll in a Ph.D. Program at Stanford. The commute was a little more challenging but now his world came into sharper focus since his full academic program targeted his true passion: Quantum computing. As a teaching assistant he would challenge students who found his passion and singular focus both challenging and entertaining. His academic papers discussing the results of his experimental research appeared in many of the leading scientific journals. His dissertation, Harnessing the Qubit, was published by Stanford's Academic Press and received considerable acclaim. Upon graduation he turned down several teaching offers from prestigious universities deciding instead to set up his own laboratory. He leased an abandoned warehouse into which he moved all the equipment from his parent's shed and began to work in earnest.

Before falling asleep Charles had been poring over a variation of Shor's quantum algorithm for integer factorization, and how exactly it interfaced with the mystical quantum realm in order to find the prime factors so much faster. His thought experiment had become exhausting and he had once again fallen asleep. Now, still drowsy and upset by the nightmare, he turned to the computer sitting on the workbench. More out of a need for distraction than anything he opened his email and was somewhat surprised to find a most curious message from someone calling himself simply AFRIEND.

"I think we share a similar passion and goal," the message read.

Normally he would have deleted the message and gone back to work but again his subconscious need for distraction prompted him instead to respond.

"Do I know you?"

After only a moment's delay, a response: "No, but I've read your academic papers and some of your posts on the physics forums and I think your ideas hold a lot of promise. Perhaps we can share thoughts that might help you to make progress."

Charles was immediately suspicious but also intrigued. Perhaps if he just asked questions without sharing too much of his own research.

"What do you have in mind?" Charles typed.

"We both know that the major stalemate for the last 20 years has been how to deal with error correction. Qubits hold the promise of unlimited speed but are entirely too accepting of the chaos of the quantum universe. If I might use an analogy, Qubits are by far the fastest horse in the race but they resist the bridle to guide them."

"An interesting analogy; I agree," Charles responded.

"You're using fluxonium Qubits, correct?" the message read.

Charles was now more tentative; this was getting too specific. Perhaps he should tell his anonymous "friend" to buzz off. But where was this going? Okay, one more response.

"Yes," he replied.

"What if the Qubits are arranged like this..." and a complex geometric diagram appeared. "To continue my analogy, this is the gate that ensures the horse can only gallop to the future desired."

Charles stared at the screen and his jaw literally dropped open. After perhaps half a minute he managed to respond: "Let me think about this. Thanks." He closed his reader.

It was as if the pieces of the puzzle he had been struggling with for years had finally fallen into place. He rushed to his whiteboard and began scribbling furiously, equations and diagrams flowing from his mind onto the board.

The breakthrough that Charles had been given was a new approach to quantum error correction.

2032

In quantum computing, errors were a persistent problem due to the delicate nature of qubits, the fundamental units of quantum information. Conventional error-correction methods were inefficient and limited the potential of quantum computers. But this new method promised to revolutionize quantum computing by drastically reducing errors and making quantum computers much more stable and reliable.

With newfound determination, Charles worked tirelessly to develop and refine his error-correction technique. He barely slept, surviving on a diet of instant noodles and energy drinks. His warehouse became a hive of activity, with cables, circuits, and trial quantum processors strewn everywhere, each with a slight variation of the geometric theme he had been shown. But Charles was undeterred. He believed he was on the cusp of achieving something extraordinary.

With the support of a few key allies, Charles embarked on a quest to secure the resources he needed to build his quantum supercomputer.

He scoured the internet for grants, scholarships, and funding opportunities. He wrote countless research proposals and grant applications, each one, he hoped, a bit more persuasive and compelling than the last. Interestingly he found grant writing to be somewhat analagous to science. He discovered that in every Request for Proposals, RFP's, there was something akin to an atomic structure with each word much like the particles in his physics experiments. Consequently he quickly learned to order these particles in the most efficient patterns possible to produce the desired element: Funding.

The breakthroughs in his error-correction technique caught the attention of a prominent tech billionaire, Richard Thornton. Thornton, who had made his fortune in the early days of the internet, was known for his interest in cutting-edge technologies. He lead a well-recognized venture capital group whose sole purpose was to identify and fund "world changing" technologies. Intrigued by Charles' work, he agreed to fund the young scientist's ambitious project.

With Thornton's backing, Charles was able to assemble a team of brilliant physicists, engineers, and computer scientists. They joined him at his warehouse in Silicon Valley and began the arduous process of building the world's first quantum supercomputer. The project was code-named "Project Quanta."

Building a quantum supercomputer was no small feat. The team faced numerous challenges, from sourcing the rare materials needed for quantum processors to developing the specialized cooling systems required to keep the qubits at ultra-low temperatures.

The warehouse was transformed into a high-tech laboratory, filled with cutting-edge equipment and a maze of cables and wires. Charles and his team worked day and night, pushing the boundaries of their knowledge and expertise. They encountered countless setbacks and failures along the way, but they refused to give up.

One of the biggest challenges they faced was the need to scale up their error-correction technique. As the quantum supercomputer grew in size and complexity, so did the potential for errors. Charles had to continuously refine and adapt his error-correction methods to keep pace with the demands of the project.

Rival research teams around the world were also working on quantum computing, and Charles knew that time was running out. He couldn't afford to lose the race to build the first successful quantum supercomputer.

Sleep-deprived and consumed by his work, Charles' health began to deteriorate. He pushed himself to the brink of exhaustion, but he couldn't slow down. The dream of quantum computing had become an obsession, and he was willing to sacrifice anything to see it realized.

Despite the challenges, the team made steady progress. The quantum processors became more stable, and the error-correction technique proved to be remarkably effective. They reached a critical milestone when their computer was able to assimilate the Bernstein-

2032

Vazarani, Quantum Phase, and Simon and Shor Algorithms flawlessly.

The next challenge: Charles input a complex problem that had stumped classical computers for decades, the Halting Problem. The Halting Problem, simply put, is a decision-making conundrum. In essence it challenges the computer to determine whether a program given a certain input will continue to run the program indefinitely or will come to a halt. The analysis, given a significantly large program, quickly overwhelms a classic computer even with massive storage capabilities. The team entered the program. The quantum supercomputer sprang into action, its qubits entangled and performing computations at speeds that were beyond comprehension.

Minutes passed, and then the quantum supercomputer produced the answer—a solution that would have taken classical computers centuries if ever to compute. The room erupted in cheers and applause as Charles and his team realized the magnitude of their achievement.

They had built the world's first successful quantum supercomputer.

Charles went to his computer to send the news to Thornton and was shocked when he opened his email account. There in his inbox was a message from someone he had not thought about in months: AFRIEND.

Tentatively Charles clicked on the message to open it and was even more shocked by the message. Two words only: "Thank you."

CHAPTER TWO

THE SENATOR

Friday, October 29, 2032—2:45 PM EDST

John Summers stood at the window of Senate Office 223 looking out at the Capitol Dome but really taking no notice. Twenty-five years in the U.S. Senate had taught him to focus on one thing only and that was the joy of acquiring power and wielding it to whatever purpose he desired. Yes, the money was rewarding—the insider trading, the cash "donations," the hilariously exorbitant speakers fees—all allowed him to live extravagantly and, in themselves, conveyed some ability to manipulate the lives of those around him. But it was the furtive glances of junior senators, the obsequious smiles of staffers, the deferential behavior of fellow committee members when he entered the room, the polite tips of the hat from policemen when they found out just whom they had pulled over that gave him the greatest satisfaction.

It had taken him almost twenty years to realize his dream of being Senate Majority Leader. Twenty years of backroom dealing, ego-stroking, and, if he were being honest, lying, cheating, bribing and extortion. But in the end it had all been worth it. He smiled as he thought to himself that Lord Upton was wrong; power doesn't corrupt, it seduces and that seduction, like all seductions, is absolutely the best thing about being alive.

"Excuse me, Senator, but you asked me to remind you of the committee meeting."

John emerged from his reverie and glanced at his aide standing in the doorway. "Thank you, Andrew; on my way."

He grabbed his attache and walked purposely into the outer office.

2032

"Andrew, confirm the dinner meeting tonight with the Pfizer VP...what was her name again?"

"Sheila MacArthur, sir?"

"Yes, Sheila...how could I forget. She was the FDA Chair for five years. Good looking gal, be nice to see her again."

"Yes sir, will confirm time and place," Andrew answered.

"Thanks, Andrew; should be back in the office in a couple of hours."

John exited the office and headed for the committee meeting in the Dirksen Office Building. He pulled his shoulders back a bit as he entered the hallway. At 63 he knew he didn't have the movie-idol looks that had successfully carried him into politics a quarter of a century before, but at six feet one with a body his personal trainer constantly insisted belonged to a man half his age, he knew he still cut what his mother would have called "a fine figure of a man." Even staffers and visitors who didn't recognize his face from his many television appearances would often do a double-take. So he enjoyed these hallway promenades immensely. He walked down the hallway to the elevator which would take him to the private subway connecting the Capitol to the Dirksen.

He entered the conference room and, as usual, the banter immediately subsided as he strode to the Chair. A quick look around the table confirmed that all members were present.

"Thank you, everyone, my apologies for being a bit late...let's get started." He smiled that smile that had successfully launched a hundred campaigns and took his seat. Everyone quickly followed suit.

"I called this closed session before tomorrow's public meeting to touch on a few details and make sure we're all on the same page. This is not a formal meeting so we'll forgo the usual rules of order. As you all know the topic of free speech is always a hot one so there will be plenty of press coverage at the meeting tomorrow. Any slip up could have profound consequences.

2032

"As long as I've been in the senate we've wrestled with the chaotic flow of information that emerged with the growth of the worldwide internet. Some of you can remember when television and newspapers conveyed information to the masses. Consequently it was quite easy to control the narrative to ensure that the people saw and heard only what we wanted them to see and hear. The internet, somewhat ironically given that it grew out of a DARPA program, changed all of that in little more than a decade. Now one could argue that television and newspapers have become almost irrelevant in how information is being disseminated.

"There have been some attempts to bring the situation back under control. The Department of Homeland Security, for example, back in the early 20's attempted to establish a Disinformation Governance Board, but a large public outcry pointing out the similarities between the Board and Orwell's Ministry of Truth quickly halted that effort.

"The FBI, CIA, NSA and other law-enforcement agencies have all made attempts to subjugate the major social media platforms in order to control the narrative. All these efforts have been in vain, in part because a rogue billionaire decided to buy a major platform and play by his own rules, and by the courts who ruled that such partnerships between social media platforms and government agencies violated the First Amendment. The intelligence agencies are still trying to by-pass the court's injunctions by using their counterparts in friendly nations as proxies but for the most part the internet is still chaotic and information, especially information we would rather control, is still flowing freely.

"I don't need to tell any of you what this has cost. There was a time when a senator was seen as not only a leader but as a paragon of virtue, an ideal. Now, according to the latest public opinion polls, fewer than 10% of the American people perceive senators in a positive light but instead see us merely as prominent players in a system that is totally corrupted by greed and special interests. And any government, but especially any democratic government, that has lost the trust of its citizenry must ask itself whether it truly holds the ability to govern.

"That's why tomorrow's committee session is so important. This new bill that we are proposing is absolutely critical if we are to retake the helm of control and right the ship of state and steer it once again back on course."

"That's a great campaign speech, Senator Summers..." John quickly locked eyes with Jean Marks, the senator from Montana, who had interrupted him, "but do you really think this bill has even a remote chance of being ratified in the chamber and, if so, that there's even a prayer of the house taking it up?"

John stared a moment at the young senator. "Of course it has a chance, Jean. We've spent the last two months conducting publicly broadcast hearings in which witness after witness has testified to the direct and indirect damage misinformation spread by various social media has caused the American people. Those testimonies have established a foundation on which we can present this bill to the senate and the American people. The key issue, as we state clearly in the bill's language, is one of public health. One of our fundamental responsibilities as lawmakers is to protect the health and welfare of the population. It is as critical to protect them from damaging misinformation as it is to provide clean drinking water."

The young senator responded with her famous smile. "Senator, have you or your staff bothered to monitor the social media's response to our committee hearings?"

"Of course, Senator Marks. And it's precisely these misinformed naysayers that demonstrate the problem which needs to be controlled."

"Let's look at some numbers," Senator Marks responded. "As you state, our hearings have been covered by the three historical television networks: NBC, CBS, ABC, as well as CNN, Fox, NPR and a few independent journalists. A recent analysis pointed out the total viewer population that could have seen those broadcasts *if every viewer chose to tune in* (a highly improbable possibility I would posit) would have been fewer than five million individuals.

"On the other hand, just *one* of those hypercritical 'naysayers' you dismiss offhand has received over twenty million views. So whose message do you think is being more broadly disseminated, which is why I ask again, do you really think the senate at large will be willing to push forward this bill?"

John responded with his own smile. "As you probably are already aware, Senator, the senate responds to its constituency, yes, but as individuals we all have sources to whom we grant, shall I say, a more open and sympathetic ear. I have shared the bill with the directors of the FBI, CIA, NSA, HSA and several other so-called three-letter agencies, and many have assured me that their agencies will do everything in their power to encourage every member of congress to give their sincere attention to our proposal. So yes, to answer your question, I do think the senate at large, and, indeed, the entire congress will respond favorably to our bill."

John looked around at the other senators sitting around the table. As he had hoped there were several thoughtful heads nodding. Only Senator Marks was smiling ruefully and shaking her head slowly.

John continued, "The thing I wanted to communicate today is the importance that we speak with one voice in tomorrow's public hearing when we put forth the bill. Do I have your support?"

"I'm afraid I will have to be a dissenting voice, Senator." It was Senator Marks, of course. "The great state of Montana has always prided itself on the right of individuals to live their lives as they see fit and the citizens of Montana are the *only* voice to which I grant an 'open and sympathetic ear.' So I'm afraid I will have to voice my concerns tomorrow about the wisdom of proceeding with this legislation."

2032

John was fuming inside but, of course, he responded only with his usual warm smile: "Of course, Senator, that's the foundation of a democracy. But we did hammer out this bill as a committee, and while you've freely voiced your disagreements along the way, we did vote in the end to proceed with submitting this bill."

"I understand, Senator," Jean responded, "but at the meeting tomorrow I will share that the bill is being submitted without a full consensus. As I have shared many times previously, this is a basic constitutional issue and I feel in my soul that this bill is a First Amendment infringement."

John finished the committee meeting insuring that all the members excepting Senator Marks were onboard, but he was still fuming inside as he rode the elevator down to the subway car that would take him back to the Capitol. Jean had been a disruptor from day one. Why was it that backwater states like Montana whose entire population could be swallowed up by one city in his home state of

California always send such idealistic troublemakers to Washington?

He exited the elevator and boarded the private subway car. He looked around and realized there were no other senators in the adjoining open-top cars. "Well, there's no use calling the directors of the FBI or CIA; they're newbies who still haven't learned how the game is played. However, I can call the directors of Homeland Security and the NSA when I get back to the office," he said out loud to the empty cars. "I'm sure that there are some skeletons in Jean's closet that can convince her to take a back seat in tomorrow's open meeting."

In less than a minute he was back under the Capitol. He was still focused on his thoughts as he exited the car and started walking hurriedly toward the elevator so didn't notice the janitor mopping until literally bumping into the yellow caution sign. At the sound the janitor, just a couple of feet away whirled with his mop. John awkwardly leaped to his left, his foot landing on the wet tiles and immediately sliding out from under him which sent him sprawling.

He hit the cold tiles hard and laid dazed. Slowly his focus returned and he realized the janitor was leaning over him looking concerned. "Lie still, sir, lie still...you took a really bad fall. I was a medic in the army. I didn't like the way your foot landed; would you mind if I just palpate your ankle before we get you back on your feet?"

John was still a bit dazed but now was beginning to be more embarrassed. "No, no, that's not necessary, just help me to my feet."

"Sir, please sir, it will just take a second. Again, I was an army medic. It will just take a second and it could prevent serious complications."

John just wanted to get up but the man seemed insistent. "Oh, okay, but make it quick."

The janitor smiled, moved down to John's left foot and gently lifted it off the tile. He placed one hand under the heel of John's foot and the other hand under his ankle and gently moved the foot sideways.

John felt a piercing pain shoot from his ankle up his calf. It caught him off guard so he had no time to control the gasp from escaping his lips.

The janitor met his eyes. "I was right." By now several people had gathered. "Just lie still, sir, and I'll call the OAP and ask them to send down a gurney." He gently laid John's foot on the tiles and made his way through the circle of onlookers and rushed away.

A young female leaned over John. "Help is on the way, sir. How are you feeling."

John looked up at her smiling face. "Embarrassed if I'm being honest, and I'm feeling really drowsy." John smiled and closed his eyes.

Ten minutes later a physician and nurse arrived from the Office of the Attending Physician. They had anticipated finding a stereotypically overweight senator whom they would strain to hoist onto the gurney and take back to the office. They were therefore quite shocked when instead they found John Summers, Senate Majority Leader, lying on the tiles quite dead.

CHAPTER THREE

THE AGENCY IS SUMMONED

Friday, October 29, 2032—7:00 PM EDST

Martin Kessler finished washing the few dishes from dinner, placed them in the drying rack and walked into the front room of his apartment. As FBI special agent in charge of the Mission Services Division of the Washington, DC field office, his simple one-bedroom apartment accurately reflects his personality. His life focus has always been his career. Growing up in the foothills of the Blue Ridge Mountains in North Carolina, his childhood had been one of hard labor and few luxuries. After graduating from the small high school near his home he received a scholarship to attend a small but prestigious university in the central part of the state where, in spite of the marginal academic training he had received in his small high school, he excelled.

After graduation from college he joined the navy. He turned down an offer to attend OCS and instead spent his senior year in college training with a Special Operations Mentor so passed his SEALS Physical Screening Test, enlisted as a Special Operator and eventually completed his SEALS training and served four years with SEAL Team Four.

He left the navy after six years and, tapping his veteran benefits, enrolled in law school. The combination of his academic and military training proved exceptionally potent. He not only was successful but made law review his second year and graduated at the top of his class. Consequently, he was actively recruited by several nationally recognized Big Law firms his final year. However, just as he had turned down the military's offer to attend OCS, Martin declined these extremely lucrative offers and instead submitted an application to the FBI which immediately accepted same. He quickly rose through his field office assignments, demonstrating an exceptional aptitude for both physical and administrative prowess, and last year had accepted his current position with the Washington regional office.

Standing just under six feet tall, 170 pounds in weight with reddish-brown hair, Martin still maintains his military physique through regular exercise. In addition to his military training he has studied both karate and Chinese boxing, holding a *nidan* ranking in the former. Ruggedly handsome, there have been women in his life but his focus on career has precluded anything serious to date which explains in part his somewhat austere lifestyle.

He walked into his small living room, turned on the TV and sat down to relax when his cellphone rang. He retrieved his phone from the coffee table, looked at the screen and immediately answered.

"Special Agent Kessler?" the voice asked.

"Yessir" Martin responded, recognizing the voice of his boss, Deputy Director Charles Lofton. "What can I do for you?"

"There has been an incident at the Capitol and I would like you to head over there immediately. Thomas Cribbs, Capitol Police Chief, is expecting you and will meet you in the Visitor's Center and bring you up to speed when you get there. You will be liaising between his department and the FBI and you will be leading a murder investigation," Lofton said. "Get up to speed and the Director and I will meet you in the Director's Office tomorrow morning at 8:00. Any questions?"

"No sir, got it; will talk with you tomorrow morning," Martin responded. He hung up, ducked into his bedroom and quickly donned his suit, tie, badge and Sig 9mm, then hurried out the door and down to the parking garage to his car.

As he headed across town he turned on the radio to see if there was any news about the incident. WTOP had a short piece reporting that

John Summers, Senate Majority Leader, had collapsed and died that afternoon. But there was no mention of murder, just a brief synopsis of his political career and a promise of more details as they became available. "Interesting," Martin thought to himself.

He arrived at the gate to the Capitol and showed the guard his badge. The guard was obviously expecting him so quickly nodded, briefly checked out the car interior and motioned him on through. He parked the car and headed into the Visitor's Center.

Cribbs met him as soon as he walked through the entrance.

"Agent Kessler, Thomas Cribbs, glad you're here. If you'll follow me let's head down to the subway and I'll fill you in on what we know at this point." The two men quickly walked to the elevator and headed for the subway. As the elevator doors closed Martin, noting they had the elevator to themselves, turned to Cribbs.

"Chief Cribbs, Director Lofton told me I would be heading up a murder investigation. I figured all Washington would be abuzz but when I checked the radio on the way over the only thing I heard was that the Senate Majority Leader had died this afternoon...no mention of foul play. What's going on?"

"Just call me Tom. Yeah, this is unfolding pretty quickly. It started out looking like a heart attack. The OAP got to the senator quickly, about 10 minutes it appears, and immediately began resuscitation efforts. But the doc noticed the pin point pupils and blue lips, suspected fentanyl, administered Naloxone, but they were unable to revive the senator. They immediately transported to Walter Reid where they did a toxicology screen and found that the senator had a lethal mixture of oxycodone and carfentanyl in his system. You familiar with it?"

"Yes, related to fentanyl but maybe fifty times stronger," Martin responded, "and my name's Martin."

"Right, thanks. No way it could have been self administered; the subject would collapse on the spot. So they went over the body with a literal magnifying glass and located a microscopic pin prick above the senator's ankle. The doc told the officer who accompanied the body to the hospital, the officer called me and I immediately called Charles."

The elevator stopped. Exiting the elevator Martin immediately located the taped off area with a Capitol Officer standing nearby. It was now a bit after 9:00 PM so there was no one else on the platform.

"Senator Summers was returning from the Dirksen Office Building when he fell here," Cribbs began. "We have the whole incident on video," Cribbs continued, pointing to the nearby surveillance camera, "but I thought you would want to see the physical site first."

"You're right, thanks," Martin responded.

"There was a janitor mopping the floor. On the video it looked like the senator was preoccupied with something, or perhaps he had already been injected. He literally ran into the caution sign, tried to regain his balance and sprawled out on the tiles. Hit the floor pretty hard," Cribbs continued. "On the video you can see the janitor trying to help him and then the senator gets surrounded by a small group of senators and their staff. The janitor rushes off and calls the OAP who, like I said, got here in less than ten minutes."

Martin hesitated as they reached the tape. "You've already completed a thorough sweep for physical evidence," he asked.

"Yeah," Cribbs answered, "literally. Like I said, we initially thought it was a simple heart attack so the responding officers took down everyone's name and a brief statement of what they saw. But then the doc noticed the symptoms, administered the naloxone, and we started treating the scene more seriously thinking it was perhaps a drug-related crime of some sort. I arrived about that time and took over the scene. Unfortunately a few of the witnesses had already wandered off but those remaining were asked to come to our office for formal statements. Those are being completed as we speak. I cordoned off the area and had our forensics team go over the entire subway platform and gather anything of interest. Unfortunately they didn't find anything of note though they're going through the meager physical evidence back at the lab."

"Excellent work, Tom," Martin responded. "I think I have a basic grasp of the scene; let's take a look at the video."

Martin and Tom took the elevator back up to the first floor, then walked down a couple of hallways to an innocuous unmarked door where Tom stopped, knocked and the door opened immediately. Martin glanced up at the nearby ceiling cameras and walked in after Tom. He walked into a huge room with every wall covered with screens with men and women in front of them constantly panning the hundreds of images. There was a constant but subdued chatter as screens were occasionally enlarged and shrunken as images were examined.

"We share this space with the Secret Service," said Tom smiling. "London has nothing on our ability to watch the Capitol and the surrounding 200 blocks. I've commandeered a small room in the back where we've got things already set up for us."

The two entered a small room on the far side of the complex. Martin thought it could have been a supply closet at one point; there was just enough room for a desk with a keyboard and what appeared to be a joystick. Above the desk was a large screen flanked by several console units. In front of the desk were three chairs on rollers. Tom took a flash drive from his pocket, inserted it in one of the consoles and sat down, motioning for Martin to take the seat next to him.

"The video begins with the senator entering from the top of the frame," Tom said as the video began playing on the screen before them. Both watched as the senator bumped into the sign, slipped on the floor and fell heavily to the tile. They watched the janitor rush to his aid and seemed to be speaking with the senator before people started rushing up to the senator from three directions. They continued to watch the video until the OAP staff arrived, the crowd parting to allow them access to the senator, and began their examination. It was easy to see the change in pace and demeanor when the staff realized the senator wasn't breathing and the intensity of the interventions escalated accordingly.

"Okay," Martin said, "there's no need to watch any further. We know the drug was obviously in his system before the OAP arrived, so let's go back and play the video from the beginning at half speed."

"Got it," Tom agreed. He worked the joystick and a couple of buttons and the video began again. Both men instinctively leaned in toward the screen as the scene repeated itself in slow motion. At the point where the senator contacted the sign Martin asked for the speed to be halved again. Tom reduced the speed but kept his hand on the joystick.

"Freeze it," Martin barked. "Can you zoom in on the janitor's mop?"

Tom did so. "Okay," Martin continued, "advance frame by frame." After a few frames Martin spoke again: "Well, it's clear that the janitor's mop never actually touched the senator; the senator clearly slipped on the wet tiles." Zoom back out and continue at half speed. They watched as the senator seemed to float in midair before landing hard, his head visibly bouncing off the tiles. "Ouch," Martin muttered.

"Quarter speed again," Martin said as people began to enter the frame. "Freeze," Martin said, with the scene now filled with perhaps a dozen people. "Back up one frame." Tom backed the scene up. Another...another..."There, lower right, just before the guy in the black suit steps into the frame, look at the woman in the white dress' legs."

"It's the janitor's shoe," Tom said.

"Right," Martin responded. "Looks like he might've been kneeling. But it proves he was obviously near the senator's ankle. Is the janitor still here at the Capitol?"

"Let me check," Tom answered. He touched his ear and muttered. "No, we got his statement," Tom continued, "and his shift was up so we sent him home."

"How about you and I pay him a visit?" Martin responded. "We can take my car."

"Sounds good," Tom replied. He touched his ear again and muttered a few sentences as both men stood. Tom cleared the screen, removed the flash drive and replaced it in his pocket and opened the door for both to leave. They walked across the huge room quickly, out the door and were, in a few minutes, speeding out the Capitol entrance with Martin driving.

"Janitor's name is Samuel Fields," Tom said still communicating with his staff. "He's been working at the Capitol for 5 years and lives in an

EAH duplex on the north side of town." He gave Martin the address.

They parked on the street in front of the duplex. "Fields is in the unit on the left," Tom stated as they walked up the short drive. Lights were on in the adjacent unit but the Fields side was dark. They walked up to the front door and Tom rang the doorbell. No answer. Tom rang it again and then opened the storm door and knocked loudly on the door. Again no response. He tried the door and it was locked.

"Maybe he stopped somewhere to eat on his way home," Tom said.

"Have you got his phone number?" Martin responded.

"Hold on." He pulled out his phone and made a call, then disconnected and punched in the numbers. He waited.

"Do you hear that?" Martin asked.

"What?" Tom answered.

"There's a phone ringing inside the house. Did you call a landline or a mobile," Martin asked.

"It's listed as his cell," Tom responded.

"Sounds like a cell," Martin responded. "Let's take a look around." Both men fished mini flashlights out of their suit pockets and started to work their way around the house. The first window was screened and locked and blocked completely by an insulated blind. They opened the gate to a small fence and checked a second window but it was also covered with a blind. Next was another window with only a lacey curtain. Martin peered in and could see that it was a small bedroom which, in the darkness, appeared undisturbed. They rounded the back of the house and moved to the back door. Also locked. However the window of the door was also covered by only a thin, gauzy curtain. Martin pressed his face to the window and peered in.

"Try calling his number again," Martin said, his face plastered against the glass. Tom hit redial.

"Got it," Martin half shouted. "His phone is lying on the floor under the hall table. That's not somewhere you would store a phone. I'm calling that probable cause that something is amiss; let's go in."

"Agreed," Tom responded.

Martin stepped back and landed a perfect front thrust kick to the door just below the lock flinging the door wide opened. Both men again switched on their flashlights and drew their pistols. Martin stepped through the door and immediately to his left to prevent silhouetting. A brief scanning of the room with his light then shouted "clear." Tom joined him in the room. They were in a small kitchen with a dining table. A hallway extended straight ahead and there was a closed door on their right.

Martin pushed the door closed behind them. "Cover the hall while I check this door," Martin whispered. He took three steps, gently turned the doorknob. When he determined it was unlocked he pushed the door open with a bang, checked the opposite corner before stepping rapidly into the room toward the corner. A small bedroom with a single bed and a rocking chair. There was a closet with sliding doors closed. He walked quickly to it and slid one door open, hitting the ultrabright setting on his flashlight as he did so which lit up the closet and room like a stage set. "Clear" he shouted.

Martin exited the room and both men started walking cautiously up the hallway now brightly lit by their flashlights. A second closed door on their right across from the hall table. Martin took a handkerchief from his back pocket, quietly reached under the table and pulled out the cellphone and laid it on the table. Martin looked at Tom and motioned for him to again watch the hall, reached down, again trying the knob before sending the door flying open and stepping into the room.

Another bedroom but this one was in complete disarray. And, lying on the floor, face down and partly covered by a blanket from the bed, was the body of a man. There was a small bathroom and walk in closet which Martin quickly cleared before returning to the body, bending down, touching the neck and confirming that not only was there no pulse but the body was quite cold.

"Body," Martin shouted. He walked quickly to the door as Tom peered in. "He's dead. Let's clear the house and call forensics." They quickly finished searching the house to confirm they were alone but had not yet called for backup when they heard the sirens as they cleared the front living room.

"Looks like he has decent neighbors," Martin muttered. They turned on the living room lights and the front stoop lights and opened the door as the officers walked up. Tom met them, showed them his credentials, explained the situation and asked them to stay but that Capitol Police and the FBI would be taking the lead on the investigation. He then called his office and requested a forensics team ASAP.

Martin meanwhile had walked back to the second bedroom to examine the body. He entered the room careful not to disturb any of the items scattered about the floor and scanned the body with his flashlight. He spotted bruises and cuts conducive of a fight but no obvious fatal wounds. One hand was covered by the blanket but the other also displayed bruising. He carefully walked out of the room.

Martin explained to forensics that he wanted a thorough sweep of the entire house including every item touched, every fingerprint, every hair. They started to work and Tom and Martin stepped out onto the stoop.

"I won't say anything official until the coroner's report," Martin started, "but I'll bet my life's savings that's your janitor lying on the floor in there and that he was lying there when he was supposedly assisting the senator on the subway platform this afternoon."

"Why do you think that," Tom replied.

"The body was cool to the touch. A body loses one to two degrees an hour and our man is close to room temperature, so I'm estimating he's been dead a minimum of eleven to twelve hours," Martin responded.

"I see," Tom answered nodding his head in agreement.

"What was the janitor's name again...Fields?" Martin asked.

"Yeah, Samuel Fields."

"Let's play a hunch. Have your people send Mr. Fields' pic to Homeland Security and let's put out a nationwide BOLO with a special focus on airports and train terminals. Tell them to feed the pic into the facial recog system ASAP."

"Why are we doing this if that's our man on the floor in there?" Tom asked.

"If I'm correct, the man we're looking for was either wearing a fantastic disguise which would be difficult to wear for a full shift OR...he was a close enough physical match from the start that he was able to pass a cursory security check. I'm betting on the latter."

"Got it," Tom responded. He made a call and relayed the information to his people on the other end of the line and replaced his cell in his pocket.

"I don't know about you," Martin started, "but my gut's telling me this is something big and it's just getting started."

CHAPTER FOUR

THE CHASE BEGINS

Saturday, October 30, 2032–8:00 AM EDST

Martin arrived at the FBI Building just in time for his scheduled meeting. It had been a long night. The Capitol Police Forensics Team packed up shortly after 2:00 AM and he had bid Tom a good night and headed straight back to his apartment. In spite of being exhausted, however, he had had to fall back on his military training to force himself to shut down and had finally managed to get a couple of hours sleep before waking to get ready for his meeting with the Director and Assistant Director. He walked into the Director's reception room right on the hour and gave the receptionist his name. He did not even have time to sit down before the door opened and Lofton walked out to meet him.

"Martin, right on time as usual. The Director is expecting us so let's go in." Lofton nodded to the receptionist who hit a button on her phone and the two men walked into the large ornate office. The Director, Margaret Sadowski, rose from her desk as the two men entered.

"Agent Kessler, thanks for joining us. I know it's been a long night, or perhaps I should say a short night as far as sleep is concerned. But I'm sure you appreciate the urgency of this case."

Martin shook her hand. "Yes, Director, I understand. And you're right about a long night but we've made some great progress in a short time."

"Excellent. Have a seat and we'll get right to it then," Sadowski responded. "Charles, you can sit there," she motioned to one of the leather chairs surrounding a small conference table, "and Agent Kessler, you can sit next to him. Can we get either of you a cup of coffee, water or juice?" Both men declined and took their seats while the Director took the chair on the side facing Martin. "Okay, Agent Kessler, you may begin."

Martin recounted the night' events. "I checked with Chief Gibbs before coming in this morning," Martin said finishing his report. "Our hunch was right about the janitor. It was he in the house and he had been dead for twelve to fourteen hours. Interestingly the cause of death was the same as the senator; a lethal injection of carfentanyl. But there was obviously a struggle and a brief fight before he died. Our theory is that the perpetrator entered the house, injected Mr. Fields, who awoke and engaged his attacker briefly before the drug took full effect. In the struggle his phone was evidently kicked out of the bedroom door and slid under the hall table which explains why the perp didn't take it with him."

"Any returns on the BOLO?" Sadowski asked.

"Yes, there's good news and bad," Martin responded. "We were also right in thinking the perp looks like Mr. Fields. Facial Recognition picked up a man at Dulles who was a 92% match. The bad news is that he caught his flight before we were able to identify him."

"Where to?" Charles asked immediately.

"Denver, Colorado," Martin responded. "He's flying under the name of John Stewart. And the destination was puzzling until we checked the schedules. It appears that Stewart headed straight to the airport as soon as he left the Capitol. We're thinking he doesn't have a passport so he took the first flight available that got him as far from Washington as possible, or perhaps he just wanted a flight of a certain time duration."

"Have you alerted the Denver Field Office?" Sadowski asked.

"Yes, but of course the plane arrived last evening. They're going through the surveillance tapes and trying to locate where he's headed. I will connect with them as soon as our meeting is finished and would like to head out to Denver if you approve."

Sadowski and Lofton exchanged glances before Sadowski turned to Martin: "Yes, approved. It's been a strange night, Agent Kessler. The CEO's of two of the largest social media platforms were killed in 'accidents' last night. I don't believe in coincidences. Given what's happened here I've assigned agents to look in to both cases. If there's a connection, your case is the genesis; it's critical we catch this 'John Stewart' as soon as possible."

"I understand," Martin responded. "I would like to get right to it. Do either of you have any further questions." Sadowski and Lofton again looked at each other before Sadowski turned her gaze back to Martin.

"No, Agent Kessler; thank you for the report and great work. We won't keep you any longer." She looked at Lofton: "Keep me posted, Charles; I want to stay on top of this."

"Yes, Director," Lofton responded as he stood up from the table. Martin stood with him and both men started for the door.

"Good hunting, Agent Kessler," Sadowski said to the departing men.

Martin turned. "Thank you, Director, I'll be in touch."

Anticipating he would receive an approval, Martin had packed his bag before leaving the apartment so he headed straight to his office. He nodded to his receptionist, Janet, as soon as he opened the door: "Any calls for me?"

"Yessir, the Denver Field Office called and Chief Gibbs from the Capitol Police just called and is on the phone," Janet responded.

"I'll take the Chief's call; route it through to my office," Martin answered as he rushed through his waiting room and straight into his office where the phone was ringing as he opened the door.

"Tom, you caught me literally walking through the door after a meeting with my director; what's up?" Martin asked.

"Morning, Martin," Tom began, "figured things would be pretty busy over there. Just wanted to tell you that I contacted our satellite office in Denver and asked them to coordinate with your office and help out any way they could. Also, got the preliminary forensics reports. Nothing much from the subway platform except the guys did find that glycerin had been added to the mopping solution Stewart was using so he was definitely planning the entire 'accident' with the senator. As far as the house is concerned, nothing of note yet but the guys say it will take at least a couple of days to get through all the evidence taken."

"Got it, Tom, good work," Martin responded. "Pass along my thanks to your people. If the team needs any help I'm sure our forensics lab would be happy to help out."

"Thanks, Martin, I'll let them know."

"I'm getting ready to head to Denver myself," Martin continued, "I've already received a call from them. I'll let them know you've instructed your folks to help out. Thanks again."

"Then I won't keep you," Tom answered. "I'll keep digging on this end. Good hunting."

Martin chuckled, "You're the second person to say that to me this morning. Give me a call on my cell if anything significant comes up; otherwise I'll talk with you when I get back." Martin hung up the phone, checked his contacts list, then dialed Chris Connors, the Denver Field Office Supervisor. After only two rings Connors picked up.

"Agent Connors."

"Chris, it's Martin. Just got back to my office after meeting with the Director. Janet said you folks had called so I'm assuming you've got some news."

"Morning, Martin. Yes, we've been on this all night. We have video of Stewart arriving at DIA.

He immediately headed to Enterprise and rented a gray Nissan compact SUV. We have the license number of course. We then contacted Denver police and asked them to check their traffic surveillance cams. They were able to track the car with a visual verification of Stewart inside and discovered that he drove out of DIA and onto I-25 south. We've notified the police departments along the interstate all the way to Las Cruces and we've also given the border patrol a heads up as well as the Colorado Highway Patrol. And finally we have a surveillance plane up as of an hour ago assisting from the air."

"Great work, Chris," Martin responded. "Any hits yet?"

"Thanks," Connors answered, "nothing yet but it's only been three hours or so since we completed all of our calls. Pretty confident we'll hear something soon."

"Excellent," Martin answered. "I'm heading your way as soon as I can catch a flight. Let me give you my personal cell number so you can contact me as soon as you have some news." Martin passed along his number. "Thanks again, Chris, talk to you soon." Martin hung up.

Martin started to ask Janet to book his flight then hesitated, and then finally sat down at his desk. "This man," he thought to himself, "has probably killed two men with a well thought out plan. He knows that every TSA agent in the country has memorized his face and that we and every other police agency in the country are looking for him. There's no way he's going to make a run for the border; that's an amateur's move." He pulled open his computer. After a couple of minutes he picked up his phone and called Lofton.

"Sir," Martin began after Lofton answered, "I need a favor. I've spoken to Connors at the Denver office and it sounds like they've got things pretty organized. However, I have a wild hunch. Connors thinks Stewart is heading south. I think that's exactly what Stewart wants us to think and I think he's heading north instead. Would it be possible to get one of our jets to fly me to our office in Havre, Montana?"

"Do you have any evidence to support your hunch? And why Havre?" Lofton asked.

"No sir," Martin responded. "Just that I think Stewart is our man, I think he's a pro, and the Wild Horse Border Crossing north of Havre is one of the most remote and isolated border crossings in the country."

Lofton was silent for a few seconds. "The Director said it this morning, that this case is a critical one not just because it involves the assassination of a senator but because it could well be the start of something truly sinister. I'll check to see if there's a plane available. If so I'll call you back in a few minutes and let you know."

"Thank you, sir," Martin responded. "I'll contact Havre and let them know I might be heading their way."

"Will call you back in a few," Lofton answered and hung up.

Martin again checked his files and placed a call to Basil Reese, Special Agent in charge of the Havre, Montana field office. A receptionist answered the phone and when Martin identified himself put him through to Reese.

"Basil Reese, Agent Kessler," Reese answered, "what can I do for you?"

"Agent Reese, I'm chasing a hunch. You received our BOLO regarding John Stewart I presume?"

"Yes I did; we went over it in this morning's briefing," Reese responded.

"Well, I'm thinking there's a possibility Stewart is heading your way, that perhaps he's going to try to slip through the Wild Horse crossing. It's just a hunch but I feel strongly enough about it that I've asked the Assistant Director for a plane to get out there ASAP. He's checking on availability right now. If he can find me a ride can I get you to meet me at the airport there in Havre?"

"Of course," Reese responded, "just let me know when you're arriving and I'll be there. While I'm waiting I'll also contact Border Patrol at Wild Horse and make sure they received the BOLO."

Martin chuckled. "You're already ahead of me. Let them know Stewart is driving a gray Nissan compact SUV." Martin gave Reese the license number. "I'll call you as soon as I get confirmation on the plane and let you know when I'm heading your way."

As soon as he hung up Janet buzzed him telling him that Lofton was on the phone and patched him through. "Just got off the phone with Havre, Sir," Martin answered, "any news?"

"They're prepping the plane as we speak," Lofton responded, "and will be ready to take off by the time you get to Dulles."

"Many thanks, sir," Martin answered, "for finding the plane but especially for trusting my hunch."

"I've known you long enough to have complete faith in your abilities," Lofton responded. "Plus given the importance of this case I thought it wouldn't be a bad idea to have a plane available even if your hunch doesn't pan out and they catch Stewart heading south. A plane will make getting him back here easier and faster."

"You're absolutely right, sir," Martin answered. "Again, many thanks. If you have no questions or additional advice I'll head for the airport." Martin said goodbye and hung up the phone. The suitcase he had packed was in his car so after bringing Janet up to speed he left the office and headed down to the underground garage. He reached his car, got in, turned on the motors and started to exit the garage and clicked on the radio.

"This just in," the radio announcer said, "Speaker of the House Emily Sparks has been identified as one of the victims in the tragic pile-up on I-66 reported earlier. There has been no official report yet regarding her condition but we have confirmed she has been rushed to a local hospital. We'll bring you more details as we get them."

Martin recalled the conversation earlier with the Director. "No coincidences," he muttered, and sped off for the airport.

CHAPTER FIVE

MONTANA

Saturday, October 30, 2032—Noon MDST

It was overcast with a light skiff of snow falling when the plane landed in Havre. Good as his word Reese was waiting for Martin at the base of the boarding ladder.

"Welcome to sunny Montana," Reese joked as Martin descended the ladder.

Martin laughed. "Sort of fits my mood. Thanks again for meeting me; any news from Wild Horse?"

"Not yet," Reese answered, "but they thanked

me for the heads up and promised to let me know if Stewart shows up. Have you had lunch?"

"Haven't eaten anything since last evening," Martin responded.

"Well, I would recommend we grab something now since the pickings get pretty slim between here and the border," Reese stated.

"Sounds good," Martin answered. "Choose any place you like."

"Let's stop by the Duck Inn," Reese suggested, "best luncheon menu in town. I eat there quite often."

"Sounds good," Martin responded, and the two men headed for the black SUV parked nearby. Martin was mildly shocked to find that not only was Reese driving a gasoline-powered vehicle but that it was an older model equipped with a big V-8 engine.

Reese noted Martin's reaction and chuckled. "Montana's a different place. Still a lot of areas where chargers don't exist." Martin smiled and nodded as they both crawled into the front seats.

Reese drove them to the restaurant and they went inside. A waitress recognized Reese and showed them to a window table. At Reese's suggestion Martin ordered the soft shell tacos while he ordered the blackened bear paw burger. The waitress took their orders and headed toward the kitchen.

"Can you fill me in on the BOLO?" Reese asked. "What did this guy do that would warrant the head office sending you to Havre in a private jet?" Martin gave Reese a synopsis of the last fourteen hours.

"Holy smokes," Reese exclaimed when Martin finished. "Assassinating a senator. I guess that does justify a lot of fuss."

"Well, it's all circumstantial at this..." Martin began, smiling as he looked out the window when he suddenly stopped talking and leaned toward the window. "Is that a hotel across the street?" he asked.

"Yeah," Reese answered looking out the window, "it's the Best Western Plus Great Northern. Why, you looking for a place to stay?"

"How many hotels are there in Havre?" Martin asked.

"I think it's about a dozen," Reese answered. "Why?"

"I know how much attention BOLO's generally receive," Martin started, "especially if they're issued two-thousand miles away. Plus, I don't know if an updated BOLO has gone out mentioning the Nissan. What's your relationship like with the local chief of police."

"It's good," Reese answered, "we get together for lunch or drinks at least once a week."

"Great," Martin continued. "How about you give him a call and ask him to have his patrol cars drive through the parking lots of every hotel in town ASAP. Have them look for a gray Nissan compact SUV with Colorado plates."

"You thinking this Stewart guy is going to stop in Havre and check into a hotel?" Reese asked incredulously.

"I'm thinking Stewart would prefer to cross the border at night," Martin answered. "And he might be tired since I figure he's been up for at least thirty-six hours or so. I'm also doubting he would choose to rest until he was close to his objective. Tell your chief to make sure the patrol cars pay especially close attention to the parking areas away from the road."

"Gotcha", Reese responded. He fished his phone out of his suit jacket pocket and made the call. Just as he finished the waitress brought their orders and the two men began eating in silence. They took their time and even ordered coffee and desert. Finally Reese's phone rang. He quickly answered. After a brief conversation he put his phone back in his pocket.

"Good news maybe," he started. "There's a gray Nissan compact SUV with Colorado plates parked in the back lot of the AmericInn out on Highway 2.

Wanna check it out?"

"You bet," Marten answered. "Maybe we just got lucky. Call the chief back and ask him to have the patrol car stay out of sight but to keep an eye on it till we get there." They left a healthy tip, paid their bill and quickly walked out to the SUV. Reese cranked the SUV and turned west out of the Duck Inn parking lot and sped through town. In less than five minutes they were pulling into the AmericInn parking lot. They spotted the patrol car sitting in a parking lot a quarter of a mile to the west.

Martin and Reese parked outside the main lobby and walked inside. Martin walked up to the receptionist desk, showed her his badge and then pulled out his phone and showed her a cleaned and enlarged photo of Stewart taken at Dulles.

"We're pursuing a criminal investigation. Is this man a guest at this hotel?" he asked.

"May I?" the receptionist asked, extending her hand toward the phone.

"Certainly," Martin responded, handing the phone to her. She enlarged the photo with her fingers and peered closely.

"I think so," she said finally, "but I can't be sure because the angle of this photo is strange. But I think it's a guest who checked in just before noon."

"Can you tell me what kind of car he was driving?" Martin asked.

The receptionist handed back his phone and went to her console. After a few seconds she responded. "Yes, here it is; Mr. Peter Jones. He's driving a Nissan, Colorado license 146 YLS."

"Not the license plate on record", Martin thought to himself, "but he could easily have stolen a new set."

"Can you tell me in what room Mr. Jones is staying?" Martin asked aloud.

"Yes, he's over in the South Wing, Room 201 next to the stairs," she responded.

"Thank you," Martin returned. "Is your manager available; I need to speak with him or her as soon as possible." The receptionist lifted her phone and punched a number, spoke briefly, then said "She'll be right out."

In less than a minute a woman appearing to be in her mid-thirties walked around the partition behind the reception desk, lifted the counter and opened the low wooden gate, and, nodding to the receptionist, approached Martin and extended her hand. "I'm Pauline Coram, Day Manager of the hotel; you asked to speak with me?"

"Yes, Ms. Coram, my name is Martin Kessler, FBI Special Agent," showing her his badge, "and this is Special Agent Basil Reese. We're pursuing a criminal investigation and we believe a suspect in that investigation is currently a guest in your hotel staying in Room 201 in the South Wing. I need your assistance in order to protect the safety of your guests."

Martin noted that Coram's back visibly straightened but she answered in a calm, professional voice:

"Certainly, what is it you need?"

"First," Martin began, "are there any guests staying in the room adjacent to and across the hall from 201?"

Coram looked at the receptionist who was obviously listening intently. Coram nodded and the receptionist went to her console and began typing. "Yes," the receptionist said, "there is a guest in the adjacent room but no one in the room across the hall."

"Excellent," Martin continued. "How many guests are in the adjacent room?"

"Just one," the receptionist answered. "I think he's a sales rep of some sort; he has the room booked for three days so there's a good chance he may be out."

"Could you give him a call?" Martin asked. "If he answers ask him to come to the lobby now; use some excuse you think will get him here with no fuss."

The receptionist called, listened for 15 or 20 seconds, then replaced the receiver. "No one answered," she said, "he's probably out on business just as I thought."

"Perfect," Martin sighed. Looking at Coram he said, "Okay, I'll need a pass key, and do you have a roll of tape I can borrow?" Coram nodded and turned and went back through the gate toward her office. Martin turned to Reese, "Basil, is your vest in your car?"

"Yes," Basil responded.

"Good, let's go get it and I need my bag." He turned to the receptionist, "We'll be right back."

The men walked to the SUV. Reese opened the back and retrieved his ballistic vest and Martin pulled out his small travel case. While Reese put on his vest Martin looked over at the South Wing of the hotel. "I checked the floor plan map on the receptionist desk. There's a staircase outside Room 201 over there," Martin began, nodding with his head, "I want you at the bottom out of sight."

"Do you need a vest?" Reese asked.

"Have a III-A in my suitcase but I'm not putting in on yet," Martin answered. "Here's my plan. I'm going to 'check in' to the room across the hall, just another businessman from out of town. I noticed the hotel has an express checkout so my guess is that Stewart will just leave by the staircase when he gets up. I'm going to try to take him outside his room in the hall."

"Why don't we just take him in the room?" Reese responded. "It's two against one."

"I considered that," Martin answered. "There's a big problem. If we just knock on the door Stewart can see us through the spy hole in the door. If we use his terrorist classification as probable cause and just enter the room with the pass key, the pass key unlocks the door with a loud snap which again gives Stewart a warning. Both scenarios are likely to end with gunfire and I really want to take this guy alive if he is our man. Being in the room across the hall will allow me to visually verify he's our man and, if so, take him down."

"I don't like the idea of you taking him on by yourself," Reese responded.

Martin smiled. "Appreciate the thought. I also have an ASP in my suitcase with my vest. Plus, I've done this sort of thing many times. But that does bring up another point; if he does come down the steps stopping him is more important that taking him alive. Got it?" Reese nodded his head grimly. "Okay," Martin continued, "you head over and take up your position."

Reese walked across the lot toward the stairs. Martin grabbed his suitcase and went back into the lobby. He took the pass key and a roll of duct tape from Coram, thanking her, then headed to the elevator and rode up to the second floor. He loosened his tie and tried to look the part of a tired salesman as he rolled his suitcase down the hall and opened the door to the room across from 201. Once inside he quickly opened the suitcase and removed his vest and collapsible baton. He took off his jacket and donned the vest, then chambered a round in his Sig 226 and replaced it in his holster. He extended the ASP baton and laid in on the bed then moved to the door of the room where he quietly pulled the latch handle down and duct taped it firmly in the open position. Finally he retrieved the baton and took his position at the door.

"Now comes the hard part," he thought to himself, "waiting."

Martin pulled a straight back chair over and placed it carefully just outside the arc of the door when opening. He sat down and placed the ASP in his lap. It was a familiar scenario. In his four years with SEAL Team Four there had been a number of reconnaissance missions requiring many hours of observation in hostile surroundings so he had learned to calm his mind and body and attune his senses to his surroundings. He had called it his predator mode and he fell into this familiar state now. The next two hours flowed by in non-time as he listened and felt until he received an oh-so-subtle vibration. He quietly rose from the chair and positioned himself at the door's peep hole.

Another twenty minutes passed before he heard the latch across the hall. The door opened slowly and a face appeared looking first directly at him, then the door opened further and a man emerged. "Definitely Stewart," Martin thought to himself. His left hand was on the door handle and the collapsible steel baton was in his right. Stewart looked down the hall, then reached back in the room and retrieved a small carry-on bag and stepped out into the hall obviously closing the door behind him as quietly as possible.

As Stewart was closing his door Martin opened his. He took three steps across the hall. With his right foot forward he brought the ASP down full force onto the back of Stewart's left knee. Martin had been trained to never use the ASP on the head or body joints but this was a special case; he wasn't concerned about permanent damage. Stewart may have heard the baton whipping though the air because

Martin saw Stewart's head beginning to turn in his direction. But it was only a millisecond before the baton made contact, severing the posterior cruciate ligament of Stewart's left leg. Stewart screamed in pain as he dropped the suitcase in his left hand and pitched forward. Martin continued his forward momentum transferring his weight to his right foot he pivoted his hip and delivered a powerful roundhouse kick into Stewart's face descending toward the floor. Stewart's head snapped backward and he tumbled to the floor unconscious. Martin followed him to the floor dropping his right knee into the small of Stewart's back and then quickly grabbing both of Stewart's arms, pulling them around to Stewart's back where Martin secured the wrists with handcuffs. Calmly and quickly Martin methodically searched the body, retrieved a Glock 43 from the holster inside the waitband below Stewart's appendix, a cell phone, the rental key and finally a curiously large ring from Stewart's front right pants pocket. With his knee still planted firmly in Stewart's back, Martin retrieved his phone from his back pocket and called Reese and asked him to bring the SUV as close to the stairway exit as possible.

"You weren't kidding about having done this before," Reese said as he walked through the door.

Martin smiled. "Sometimes it doesn't go so smoothly. Help me roll him over. He's not going to be able to walk so we're going to have to carry him down and put him in the SUV."

"You want to call for help?" Reese asked.

"No," Martin answered, "help means complications. I want to get this man back to Washington ASAP. We'll put him in the SUV and take him straight back to the plane."

"Doesn't he need medical attention; his face is pretty messed up," Reese answered, as they turned Stewart over.

"He has a strong pulse," Martin answered. "He'll get the attention he needs in Washington."

"Got you," Reese responded, noting the change in Martin's face. This was not the agent who got off the plane earlier and with whom he had eaten lunch. This was the face of a hardened soldier.

The men carried Stewart down and placed him horizontally in the back seat of the SUV. Martin then returned upstairs and using the pass key thoroughly searched Room 201. The only thing he found was the room key Stewart had left on the dresser. He then went across the hall, removed the tape from the door and returned the room to its previous state, repacked his vest and baton and carried his suitcase down to the SUV. They drove back to the front entrance where Martin went in, returned the two room keys and duct tape and thanked the manager and receptionist for their assistance.

"Let's check out the Nissan," Martin said, opening the passenger door of the SUV, glancing in at the back seat and then sitting down. They drove through the lot in front of the hotel but didn't spot anything then circled out to the access road and pulled into a lot on the opposite side of the south wing. The Nissan was parked in the back corner of the lot. Martin got out of the SUV and quickly went through the vehicle finding nothing but discarded wrappers from a fast food joint and a half-eaten bag of Doritos. He locked the Nissan and walked back to the SUV and climbed in.

"Have your people come out and pick up the Nissan after I lift off and go through it a bit more carefully. Don't think there's anything there but if you do find something send it to the lab in DC," he said handing the Nissan key to Reese. "Let's get back to the airport as quickly as possible."

Reese pulled the SUV out on the access road and accelerated rapidly. Martin pulled out his phone and dialed Lofton's number.

"Sir, it's Martin..." he started when Lofton answered.

"Martin," Lofton interrupted, "I was just about to call you. All hell's breaking lose here and I'm really hoping you're making progress."

"That's why I'm calling, sir," Martin answered. "We've got Stewart. He's in the back seat of our SUV and we're on the way to the airport."

"Great news, finally," Lofton answered, "is he alive?"

"A little the worse for wear," Martin replied chuckling, "and he won't be walking anytime soon, but he's alive. You said all hell's breaking lose; what's going on?"

"In the last ten hours two congressmen, three senators, and the heads of Homeland Security and the NSA have all been murdered," Lofton replied gravely. "I've got the Director sequestered as much as she will allow with a 24/7 security team assigned to her. And that's just the tip of the iceberg. Get that man back here ASAP and I'll fill you in with the details. Got to go," and he disconnected.

Martin sat silently with the phone in his hand as Reese pushed the SUV west on Highway 2 toward the airport. Reese glanced over at him then asked "what was that about hell breaking lose."

"War," Martin answered calmly, "I think we're at war."

CHAPTER SIX

EXPANSION

Sunday, October 31, 2032-1:00 AM EDST

The plane rolled to a stop inside the private hanger at Dulles. Martin glanced at Stewart and confirmed he was still unconscious. The crew had converted two of the seats into a bed and they had strapped Stewart in. Reese had pulled in an EMT from the airport's emergency response team who had examined Stewart, confirmed he probably had a torn ligament and perhaps a damaged cervical vertebra but was in stable condition. The EMT had also administered a sedative to ensure Stewart would remain unconscious for the duration but Martin had made sure the straps were tight and had handcuffed one of Stewart's wrists to the seat frame just to be safe. Seeing that Stewart was still secure Martin grabbed his bag and Stewart's, moved to the front of the plane and descended the boarding steps. An Op Med Team was already at the base of the steps and raced up the steps with a portable gurney as soon as he stepped off. Martin walked over to Lofton who was standing twenty feet away.

"Welcome back, Martin," Lofton said solemnly, "and congratulations again. I can't tell you how important your capturing Stewart may be."

"Thank you, sir," Martin responded. "This is everything Stewart had with him," he added, extending the small suitcase toward Lofton, "we probably should get this to Forensics ASAP." Lofton turned to one of the four men behind him, motioned with his hand and the man stepped forward and took the suitcase. "Now sir," Martin continued, "you said on the phone that you would fill me in on what's happening."

"Sure thing," Lofton responded, smiling for the first time. "Let's head back to the office and I'll brief you along the way."

"My car's in long-term parking," Martin answered, "you want me to follow you back?"

"Not necessary," Lofton responded, "your car's already back at headquarters. You can ride with me."

Martin put his suitcase in the first SUV and he and Lofton got into the rear seat. Two of the men with Lofton got into the front seats while the remaining two put Stewart's suitcase in the second SUV then entered the front seats. As the two SUVs eased out of the hanger Martin watched the Med Ops people load Stewart into the back of a nearby ambulance.

"In the last thirty-six hours," Lofton began as soon as the SUVs cleared the gate, "there have been at least fifteen thousand assassinations around the world. I say at least fifteen thousand; that's all we can confirm. As you can imagine it's difficult getting accurate news from many of the countries. And all of these assassinations are people of extremely high importance: Heads of state, senators, congressmen, prime ministers, heads of intelligence agencies, CEO's of major corporations, etc.. And all but a very few of these assassinations, at first glance, appear to be accidents or death by natural causes. And those numbers were valid when I left the office; new reports are coming in on a regular basis."

"Good grief," Martin exclaimed. "You said on the phone that the heads of Homeland Security and the NSA were among those victims. What are NSA and the CIA picking up; do we have any of idea of who's behind this?"

"Nothing solid at this point," replied Lofton. "A joint task force comprised of representatives from Homeland, NSA, CIA, DOD, and the FBI is being assembled. You, by the way, are on that task force thanks in no small part to your work over the last thirty-six hours. Every agency is working on the problem and the first order of business when we convene at 10:00 AM this morning is to share what we've learned and to map out a cooperative strategic and tactical response."

"What about the Director?" Martin asked.

"As I noted on the phone I've assigned a special security team to be with her 24/7," Lofton responded. "As you can imagine she's not too happy about that. But she will be joining you and me at the task force meeting this morning. For the time being we're taking a proactive protective response. The Director's family and mine have been moved to safe houses as a precaution though it seems that none of the attacks so far have involved family members. And that's why we're headed to headquarters now. I know you haven't had much sleep over the last forty-eight hours so we've set up an apartment for you at the FBI Building. It's not the Ritz but I can guarantee it's secure. So your assignment for the next eight hours is to get as much sleep as possible before this morning's meeting."

"Thank you, sir," Martin responded. "What about Stewart and his belongings?"

"He's being taken to a secure medical facility for treatment and we're hoping to have him ready for questioning by the time we finish our meetings. His effects are being taken to the lab for immediate processing. Any more questions?"

"I'm sure there will be after I've had a chance to think about this," Martin answered, "but I can't think of anything right now. Thank you, sir."

"Oh no, Martin," Lofton replied, "thank you. Capturing Stewart may be the best news we've gotten since this whole mess began. And thanks for emailing the report on Stewart's capture; the director and I have already been over it. Once again, great work. How about food, when was the last time you ate?"

Martin chuckled. "Had a big lunch and a protein bar on the flight in but I'm not that hungry."

"You need to keep up your strength," Lofton responded smiling. "The cafeteria has been instructed to stay open 24/7 for the interim so give them a call and order anything you want once you get settled in to your quarters."

"Thank you, sir," Martin replied. "Right now I can't think of anything more attractive than a warm bed."

"Coming up," Lofton answered. "I'll show you to your room as soon as we get to headquarters; you're next door to my quarters. You can hit the sack and we'll meet with the director at nine and prep for the task force meeting."

The two men sat in silence for the remaining half hour before arriving at the FBI Building. Martin grabbed his bag and followed Lofton into the building noting the guards with MP5's just inside the entrance as they walked in. Lofton took him up to a hallway right off the mezzanine. Another armed guard at the hallway's entrance. They walked down the hallway until Lofton stopped in front of a bathroom door on their left.

"This is the shared bath," Lofton explained, "men to the left and women to the right. It's the only one in the building that has showers intended for use by the people using the running track around the mezzanine."

They walked another twenty feet to the next door on the same side of the hall. "This is the Director's quarters," Lofton continued, "mine are across the hall." He pointed to the door opposite. "Yours is the next door on the left." They walked to the next door and Lofton opened the door. "Like I said before," he continued, "it's basic but it's secure."

Martin stepped into the room. This had obviously been someone's office a few hours before. All the office furniture had been removed and replaced with a single bed and nightstand; there was a small writing desk in one corner with a desk lamp. A cardboard chest of drawers and wardrobe sat in the opposite corner.

"I know you were probably traveling light," Lofton said, "and will want to go to your apartment to pick up some additional clothes. You can do that after our meeting later. We have a guard watching your apartment but until we figure out what's going on the Director and I thought it best you join us here."

"No worries," Martin responded, "I understand. And this will do fine."

"Excellent," Lofton replied. "I'll let you get to sleep, then. We'll meet in the Director's room up the hall at 9:00. Again, the cafeteria's number is on the desk over there; give them a call if you want something to eat."

"Got it," Martin responded. "Thank you; think I'll get some shut-eye first." Lofton left and Martin quickly unpacked his bag, walked up to the bathroom and brushed his teeth, came back and plugged in his phone, set the alarm, undressed and crawled into bed. In less than two minutes he was asleep.

CHAPTER SEVEN

IT GETS DARKER BEFORE THE LIGHT

Sunday, October 31, 2032—9:00 AM EDST

Martin had awakened at 8:00, showered, shaved and then ordered an omelet, toast and coffee from the cafeteria. He got dressed and walked up the hall and stopped outside the Director's door and knocked. There was a short pause and Lofton opened the door.

"Come in, Martin," he said smiling, "were you able to sleep in your new quarters?"

Martin entered. The room was a bit larger than his accommodations. There was the same single bed and cardboard furniture but there was room for a small table able to seat four in addition to the desk. The Director was seated at the table and smiled at him as he entered.

"Yes sir," he responded, "thank you. Went right to sleep as soon as I hit the sack."

"Excellent," the Director interjected, "why don't you and Charles have a seat and we'll get started." The two men joined the Director at the table. "Charles, why don't you begin."

Lofton opened a folder in front of him. "We've gotten a preliminary report from Forensics. Stewart's real name is Paul Shore. He's a former serviceman, Air Force, where he served as a Cyber Systems Specialist for his entire four-year hitch. After leaving the Air Force he's held a number of IT jobs and for the past two years has run a small IT Security company in Denver. Has never been in any trouble that we can find, not even a parking ticket. As Martin knows, he had a phone on him and there was a tablet in his suitcase. The phone turned out to be a burner with nothing incriminating on it except one phone call to a number that is now out of service. That call was made yesterday after he landed in Denver. The tablet, on the other hand, proved more interesting. The folks in Forensics say they have just broken through the first layer but have found out that he's using Tor as his browser."

"And Tor is?" the Sadowski asked.

"It's like Chrome or Microsoft Edge," Lofton responded, "but it's open source and much more secure. It advertises itself as being completely secure which it is for the most part. Most of the developed countries intelligence folks, however, have found a way. But it gives the user access to what is commonly called The Dark Web where a user can find just about anything...and I mean *anything* for sale. Forensics said one of the things they find both interesting and challenging is that Shore downloaded the Linux version and has modified the code. In essence he has created his very own personal and unique internet browser and so far they've been unable to get to the source code to see how it works. At this point, however, I think this is a significant clue. I believe this may be strong circumstantial evidence of an internet link to our crimes."

"Very good," Sadowski said. "Anything else."

"Just that Shore is in stable condition and in isolation and is refusing to say anything." Lofton turned back a page in his folder. "He has a severed posterior cruciate ligament in his left leg and a fractured cervical vertabra but is expected to fully recover. He should be physically able to be interrogated later this morning."

"Martin," the Director continued, "Charles and I will be the face of the agency at the meeting this morning but I'm wanting you to be the spear point. I'm going to ask you to make a report for the agency at the meeting. You can give a brief synopsis of the senator's assassination and Shore's capture including the information Charles has just shared. And then I will make it clear that you're our chief investigator and will want you to be included in whatever interagency efforts take place going forward. Are you okay with this?"

"Yes, Director," Martin responded. "Thank you."

The Director smiled. "No, thank you; you're doing an exemplary job and I'm confident you won't disappoint. By the way, when it's just Charles, you and I, please call me Margaret, okay?"

Martin returned the smile, nodding, "Yes... Margaret and thank you again."

"Okay," the Director continued, "to avoid the appearance of any agency having an advantage the meeting is being held at the Capitol. Due to the assassinations Congress has called a recess. They said it is to honor their fallen colleagues but I suspect they're all frightened and have run home so there are plenty of meeting rooms available. Why don't we head on over."

The three rose and the Director put on a light jacket before she opened the door and they stepped into the hall where they were met by a four-man security team. They all walked to the elevator and descended to the sub-basement to the underground parking garage. Waiting for them were three armored SUV's. Martin noted the lead and trailing SUV's had four men each, all wearing tactical gear. Two of the men in the security team got in the lead and trailing SUV's and the remaining two, after opening the rear doors and allowing the Director, Lofton and Martin to slide inside, closed the doors and slid into the front seats.

"Ready to roll, Director," the driver said.

"Proceed," the Director responded and the driver touched his ear and whispered quietly and the three SUV's accelerated quickly through the garage and out onto the street where they were joined by a motorcycle escort. They sped toward the Capitol.

CHAPTER EIGHT

THE TASK FORCE

Sunday, October 31, 2032—10:00 AM EDST

The first thing Martin noted was that the meeting was being held in a SCIF; Sensitive Compartmented Information Facility. These were ultra-secure rooms used by congress to discuss matters of the highest national security. They were asked to give up their phones and other electronic devices before entering. The second thing Martin noticed as they entered the room was the Vice President seated at the head of the table. Tulsa Kalani, a native Hawaiian, had a reputation for being a hard-hitting, no-nonsense politician with a penchant for angering her own party as often as the opposition because she demonstrated little patience with political games. This trait, however, was greatly appreciated by the general public and it was generally conceded that choosing her as his running mate had been a major factor in the current President's election.

Seated next to the Vice President were several men and women in military uniforms, one being Vice Admiral Pulanski who had served with Martin on Seal Team Four. They made eye contact and nodded as Martin took his seat beside Sadowski and Lofton. Seated beside Pulanski was Judy Alcott who had been named Director of the CIA about the same time Martin had moved to Washington. Interestingly Martin, Pulanski and Alcott had worked a mission together when Martin was with Seal Team Four. She caught his eye and smiled warmly and nodded as well. As he looked around the table Martin recognized a couple of other faces from television interviews. The door opened behind Martin and two more people whom Martin did not recognize entered the room; one, a tall African-American man and the other a stunningly beautiful Asian woman. They took their seats and the Vice President rose.

"Good morning, everyone," she began, "thank you for coming in on a Sunday morning. It's obvious to all of us I think that we are facing an unprecedented threat to our country, indeed, to the world, which is precisely why this task force has been called. Thank you again for responding to that call. I know historically that inter-agency rivalries are as much a part of Washington culture as political fundraisers but the President and I ask that those rivalries, for this group, be put aside for the greater good. Most of you know me so know that I honor the truth above all; it's one of my personality traits that makes me so adored." She smiled and there were several chuckles around the table. She stopped smiling and leaned forward, resting her hands on the table. "So I will add this truth: If anyone sitting at this table is unwilling to work as a team with everyone here and consequently demonstrates that unwillingness in any way, I will do everything in my power to see that your agency will be so strapped for funding that your top priority for the next decade will be where to hold your weekly bake sales. I know many of you have suffered personal losses and you want to catch the persons responsible but I would remind you that working together, as an unified team, will best enable us to do just that."

"Okay," she continued after a poignant pause, "enough of my usual sweet talk. This morning's agenda is for each agency rep to introduce yourselves and then tell us what you know about the deaths that have taken place around the world over the last thirty-six hours and what your agency has learned."

The DoD representatives were the first to respond but had done little in terms of identifying who might be behind the mysterious deaths. They did, however, share two revelations. Firstly, the Chair of the Joint Chiefs of Staff who had died of an apparent heart attack while golfing at Santee-Cooper Country Club the day before was, after further investigation, confirmed to be one of the victims. His pacemaker had been hacked while out on the course. Secondly, the heads of each service had all made personal contacts with their counterparts in Russia, China and elsewhere and were convinced that all of the countries contacted were experiencing the same bizarre assassinations as the US was seeing.

Homeland Security reported next. Their Secretary of Homeland Security had been one of the few American victims who actually suffered an openly violent attack. He had been stabbed to death outside his home in Alexandria while walking his dog through their historically quiet and safe neighborhood. Homeland was, of course, throwing all of its resources into the investigation but so far their only lead was taken from a neighbor's smart doorbell showing a figure wearing a hoodie along the same street at approximately the same time the attack occurred. At this point forensics had not found any incriminating evidence from the crime scene. A middle-aged Asian man stood up.

"My name is Dr. Charles Park, Assistant Director of Homeland Security and currently appointed as Acting Director," he began. "As I'm sure everyone appreciates, things are somewhat hectic at Homeland. We are accutely focused on finding the former director's assassin, of course. However, we are pleased to report that we were able to be of some support in assisting Agent Kessler's apprehension and arrest of Senator Summers' assassin. We will continue our search for our Director's attacker and stand ready to assist everyone here in any way we can." He sat down.

"Thank you, Director Park," the Vice President responded, "and let me add my personal condolences to you and everyone at your agency for your loss."

The CIA's report was similar to the DoD. Director Alcott noted that the "chatter" and reports from agents in the field confirmed that every developed country on the globe was experiencing the same phenomena. Even so-called Third-World countries, she reported, were not immune as many tribal chiefs and strong-handed dictators had been assassinated. These assassinations, however, were atypical in that they were all violent in nature but interestingly none of the perpetrators had yet been apprehended or even identified.

Now it was Martin's turn. Sadowski made a short introduction and then handed off to Martin who gave the Task Force a synopsis of the senator's assassination and the subsequent hunt for and apprehension of Stewart/Shore.

"Our next step will be to begin the immediate interrogation of Mr. Shore when we conclude our meeting," Martin concluded. "As noted we suspect the trail lies on the Dark Web."

"Thank you, Agent Kessler," the Vice President responded. "On behalf of all of us, indeed the country as a whole. The importance of you having provided us with our first suspect in this baffling and frightening case cannot be overstated. And now I would like to hear from the representatives of the National Security Agency. I'll repeat the condolences I offered to Homeland at the loss of the Director of National Security and thank both of you for being here this morning."

The tall African-American man who had entered the room last with the Asian woman stood up.

"Thank you, Vice President Kalani, for your kind words. My name is Lamar Smith and I am currently the acting Director for the agency until the President appoints a formal Director. I would like to introduce Dr. Mei Lin who is the Director of Cyber Security for the Agency who will make our report. Dr. Lin."

Dr. Lin took a tablet from her bag and stood. "Good morning everyone," she began. "First I also want to thank the Vice President for allowing me to bring my tablet into a secure meeting; it will make my presentation much easier to follow." She pulled a small projector from her bag and placed it beside her aimed at the wall behind. "Could we dim the lights a bit please?"

The Vice President nodded to the guard at the door who darkened the room.

2032

"I asked 'Casper' to take a look at the situation," Dr. Lin began...

"Excuse me, Dr. Lin," the Vice President interrupted, "I suspect everyone knows who or what 'Casper' is but for the sake of clarity could you explain?"

"Certainly," Dr. Lin continued, "as you may know the first quantum computer to go operational in late 2029 was invented by Dr. Charles Westwood and is still in operation at Dr. Westwood's corporate facility outside Palo Alto California. And our society has already reaped many rewards from that invention in every scientific and social field one can name. However quantum computers are exceptionally difficult to design, build and, perhaps most importantly, to run. Consequently here we are three years later and there are only two operational computers in China, one in Russia, one in Japan, and one being operated by the EU in Cern, Switzerland. The United States has three: The original in Palo Alto, a second at the National Institutes of Health, and the third located at the NSA Headquarters Building in Fort Meade, Maryland. Our computer is called the Quantum Analyzer of Systems and Personnel, or QASP which we nicknamed 'Casper' in part because its purpose is to see but not be seen."

"Thank you, Dr. Lin," the Vice President interjected, "please continue."

Dr. Lin nodded and turned on her tablet and projector, turning to assure the auto focus function was working properly. "I asked Casper to take a look at our problem and to give me his thoughts. These are his first observations." She pulled up the first slide: A world map. She touched her tablet and the map was suddenly covered with tens of thousands of red dots.

"Each red dot," she began, "represents a confirmed assassination. As has been stated previously this is truly a world-wide attack. Casper pointed out that ninety-six percent of the recognized nation-states have suffered confirmed losses. The remaining four percent could also have been affected but lack of infrastructure makes it impossible for him to confirm."

She pulled up the next slide which was simply a statement: THERE IS A COMMONALITY AMONG THE VICTIMS IN THAT THERE IS DEMONSTRABLE EVIDENCE THAT EACH OF THE VICTIMS HAVE CAUSED GREAT HARM TO THEIR FELLOW HUMANS.

There was an immediate clamor from many of the people sitting around the table until the Vice President once more slapped the table. She said nothing but just glared at the individuals before finally nodding to Dr. Lin to continue.

"I asked Casper for clarification on this statement. His reply was that every victim had recommended that an unauthorized military action or war take place and/or capitalized on such an action, or had caused physical or economic damage to a significant number of people, or had used their social or political position to achieve personal economic or political gain through the financial or physical exploitation of hundreds or even thousands of their fellow humans." Dr. Lin paused a second then added, "I appreciate your emotional reaction and would merely add that our agency's director was one of the victims, and that these are Casper's observations not mine personally."

Dr. Lin brought up the next slide. It appeared to be a copy of a web page in an unusual language. "Kill lists in several less common languages have appeared on the previously mentioned Dark Web," Dr. Lin stated, glancing at Martin and smiling briefly. "They list the names of individuals, many of whom have subsequently been identified as victims, and offer bounties paid in Bit Coin for confirmed elimination. These lists identify the victim and give a phone number to be called if interested. Casper reported that he had to spoof a pay phone in the appropriate country before the phone was answered but that when he did so he was given a place and time to meet someone who would provide information to assist in the assassination. We asked a sister agency to send a field agent undercover. He arrived at the designated location and found only a note stating, and I quote, 'The NSA is ineligible to participate in this program.'"

The Vice President raised her hand. "Yes, Vice President?"

"My apologies for interrupting again, Dr. Lin, but can the NSA not shut down the web sites?" the Vice President asked.

"We can and have," Dr. Lin answered, "but I would point out some problems with this. First, it's difficult to do so without root authorization at the server being used. Of course difficult is not a significant issue for the NSA. But we would prefer that as few people as possible know that we have this ability. Secondly, when we do take action the site reappears within minutes on another server."

"Thank you," the Vice President responded. "Please continue."

"I asked Casper for likely suspects," Dr. Lin stated, bringing up the third slide, and this was his response."

ASSASSINATIONS IN DEVELOPED COUNTRIES DEMONSTRATE DETAILED KNOWLEDGE OF THE VICTIMS PERSONAL AND PROFESSIONAL ROUTINES INDICATING THE ASSASSINS HAD BOTH TIME AND INFORMATION AND PERHAPS ASSISTANCE. GIVEN THE LARGE NUMBER OF ASSASINATIONS IN SUCH A BRIEF TIME FRAME AND THAT ALL NATION-STATES HAVE SUFFERED LOSSES WOULD POINT TO A ROGUE MULTI-BILLIONAIRE OR PERHAPS A SMALL CADRE OF SUCH INDIVIDUALS.

"I followed this answer with an additional question," Dr. Lin continued, "Looking at the electronic communications of all such individuals around the world can you identify a prime candidate?"

Dr. Lin pulled up the final slide which was a name instantly recognized by everyone in the room: NOEL ATTAR "This concludes my report," Dr. Lin stated and sat down.

The Vice President nodded to the guard and the room lights brightened.

"I resent the defamation of the former Secretary of Defense's name," Vice Admiral Pulanski stated firmly.

The Vice President responded quickly. "First, the only individuals who will ever see that statement are sitting around this table Vice Admiral; fellow members of the team about which I spoke earlier." She continued to look directly at Pulanski's eyes. "Second, are you intimately familiar enough with the former Secretary's military record to make such a statement?" The Vice President then looked around the table at everyone. "Do I need to repeat myself?" she asked rhetorically. She then looked at Dr. Lin. "Thank you very much for your report, Dr. Lin, and again my condolences for the loss of your agency's director. Here are my recommendations for action, people: Agent

Kessler, you and Dr. Lin will carry out the interrogation of our only suspect. Secondly, as I noted in my phone calls last night, Directors Sadowski, Park, Smith and Alcott will join me now in a meeting with the President to give him a sitrep and report. Everyone else will compile everything your respective agencies have on Noel Attar. I trust that I do not need to remind you that Mr. Attar, aside from being one of the richest individuals on the planet, is a highly-respected and honored citizen of this country so I expect each and every one of you to display discretion and respect in your queries. Are there any further questions?"

The Vice President looked around the table at each individual. "Very well, let's all meet back here tomorrow at the same time. Till then I wish you all good hunting." She stood which signaled everyone to begin filing out of the room.

Martin, Margaret and Lofton remained seated as did Lamar and Dr. Lin, Director Alcott and Director Park. When the room had cleared everyone rose and walked toward each other and were joined by the Vice President.

"I want to thank both of you again for your work," the Vice President said, looking at both Martin and Dr. Lin. "If there's anything my office can help you with in your interrogation please let me know." She then looked at the others. "The President and I will expect the Directors to join us as as quickly as possible at the White House." She nodded and left the room with Directors Park and Alcott following.

Margaret stepped forward and offered her hand to Lamar. "Again, let me add my condolences for your agency's loss, Mr. Smith" as they shook hands, "and to you Dr. Lin" and they shook hands as well. "How would you like to coordinate the interrogation?"

"Thank you very much," Lamar responded. He looked at Dr. Lin. "Dr. Lin?"

"Would it be possible to conduct the interrogation at our facility?" Dr. Lin began. "I realize this would be an inconvenience but I would like to elicit Casper's assistance in the process and I think he could be of immeasurable help, especially if the subject is as uncooperative as I would expect him to be."

Margaret looked at Martin. "He's your suspect, Agent Kessler; any objections?"

"He's in a secure medical facility with some fairly serious injuries," Martin answered. "Can you provide the necessary medical support?" he asked turning to Dr. Lin.

"Yes, I think we can," Dr. Lin responded. "The East Campus Building has an infirmary equipped to handle medical emergencies and even includes an operating theater. Just tell us what you need and we'll have it available."

"Then I don't see any objections," Martin continued. "If you'll give me the name and phone number of your medical officer I'll have our medical team make the call and coordinate the transport."

"Excellent," Dr. Lin answered, giving Martin a warm smile. She took her tablet from her bag, quickly pulled up a screen and gave the name and number to Martin. "When can we begin?"

"Let's step outside the SCIF," Martin said and walked out into the corridor. He retrieved his phone and called the medical facility, spoke briefly, then walked over to where the others had gathered. "Our team is contacting your folks as we speak. They said we should be able to have Shore in Ft. Meade within two to three hours."

"Great work, Agent Kessler," Margaret responded. "Director Smith and I need to get to our meeting but why don't you and Dr. Lin have lunch and get acquainted since you'll be working together?"

"Are you free for lunch, Dr. Lin?" Martin asked. "I need to check with our forensics folks who've been working on Shore's phone and tablet so would like to head back with the Assistant Director, but I could meet you someplace."

"Certainly," Dr. Lin answered. "And could you transport the phone and tablet with Mr. Shore; I'm sure Casper would love to take a look."

The two decided on a luncheon site while Margaret and Lamar left for their vehicles. Then everyone remaining said their goodbyes and headed out to their respective cars.

"Excellent job with presentation, Martin," Lofton said as they rejoined their support vehicle and headed back to headquarters. "Are you comfortable working with Dr. Lin?"

"Thank you, sir," Martin responded. "Yes, Dr. Lin seems pleasant enough though I find it... interesting how she has anthropomorphized their computer system. Have you had any experience with Casper before?"

"Not personally," Lofton answered, "the NSA is perhaps the most tightly closed shop in Washington. But I have heard some interesting rumors about their computer system. I'm sure that was one reason the Director was open to the proposal to conduct the interrogation there; we'll be very interested in hearing your report."

The motorcade pulled into the FBI underground garage. "If you will excuse me, sir," Martin said, "I think I'll call Quantico and check on how they've gotten along with the tablet and phone and then have them courier the items over to Ft. Meade. I'll contact the Director and you as soon as I get back from the interrogation."

"Certainly," Charles answered, "and enjoy your lunch." Charles walked toward the elevator and Martin walked to where Charles had told him his car was parked. He got to his car, unlocked it and got in and made his call to Frank Vestal, the chief lab tech who was working on the Shore evidence.

"Frank, Martin," Martin began, "have you made any progress on the phone and tablet?"

"Nothing additional on the phone," Frank responded, "but we've made a good deal of progress with the tablet. I think we've figured out his coding. Shore cleared his cache but we recovered the web site from which he purchased the oxycodone/carfentanyl, so you've got pretty solid evidence there. Oh, by the way, that ring you brought in...it's a micro-injector; that's how he delivered the solution. Again, solid evidence. But the big news comes from the tablet's hidden files. You're not going to believe this."

"What did you find?" Martin asked.

"Shore was emailed a detailed plan for the attack on the senator. Everything was spelled out. The janitor's address, when he would receive the false id's, where he needed to be mopping and when, the flight to Denver, the number to call when he got there, when to cross the border and where, everything! The number to call, by the way, was the number on his burner phone. We also found a second file confirming a bit coin account in Shore's name with a balance of the equivalent of $20 million."

"Wait a minute," Martin responded incredulously, "you're telling me Shore planned the flight to Denver *before* the day of the attack?"

"Yes," Frank answered, "and that's not the spooky part. We checked. The flight to Denver was *delayed* thirty minutes. Otherwise, Shore would have gotten to the airport too late to catch it."

"Sheesh, you're right," Martin responded, "that's beyond spooky. Great work, Frank. Listen, Frank, we've moved the interrogation to the NSA headquarters in Ft. Meade. Could you have an armed courier bring the phone and tablet up with instructions to hand deliver only to either me or a Dr. Lin? Need this done ASAP."

"Hold on a second," Frank responded, "let me put you on hold." After a minute he was back on the line. "Sure thing; he's leaving now."

"Fantastic work, as always, Frank," Martin answered. "Thanks my friend. Beers are on me next time you're in town."

"No problem, Buddy," Frank answered chuckling, "and I'll definitely take you up on the beers. Good luck with the interrogation." He hung up and Martin sat in his car thinking. "Curiouser and curiouser," he thought to himself. He called Charles and gave him a synopsis of the forensics report and asked if he could have someone find out more details on why the flight was delayed. Then he took a deep breath, turned on the motors and drove out of the garage.

CHAPTER NINE

THE BRIEFING

Sunday, October 31, 2032—Noon EDST

The Vice President's motorcade was the first to arrive at the White House, followed within minutes by the motorcades of Directors Alcott and Park. Director Sadowski's motorcade and Director Smith's motorcade were the last to arrive. Security at the White House, as expected, was intense; all the motorcades passed through two checkpoints before reaching the formal gates and being admitted. Upon arrival everyone was shown to the White House Family Dining Room where a luncheon had been set up.

As everyone arrived they were served the drink of their choice and all elected to stand and talk informally awaiting the President's arrival. They had been chatting for only a few minutes when he walked through the door flanked by two secret service agents who, after briefly surveying the room, took up posts on either side of the door.

Vivek Gadani had been elected by a significant majority in the 2028 election. He had been a successful businessman before entering politics. Interestingly, he and the Vice President would have been sitting on opposite sides of the aisle a decade earlier. However both had always been outspoken critics of Washington's corruption and, before the 2028 election, had decided to head an independent party whose primary platform had been to address and correct that corruption. With the 2032 election only a week away, the polling numbers put them both at least twenty points ahead of the candidates of the other parties. Though there were differing opinions on how successful they had been in their efforts over the last four years, it was obvious that their message and efforts were greatly appreciated by a vast majority of Americans.

President Gadani walked across the room, a somewhat grim smile on his face, and extended his hand to the Vice President. "Thank you, Tulsa, for pulling this meeting together on short notice." He then turned to the directors, shaking each director's hand, before extending his hand toward the set table and asking everyone to find a seat. When everyone had been seated he took his seat at the head of the table, turned to the secret service agents and nodded his head. The agent on the right side of the door raised his hand to his face and spoke quietly and in just a few seconds the wait staff started rolling their carts into the room.

"I hope everyone is okay with chicken breast and vegetables," President Gadani said, "there wasn't a lot of time to prepare anything fancy."

Everyone nodded their heads and smiled as the wait staff set a service in front of each person, asked if there was anything else needed, then quickly left the room.

"Okay," President Gadani began, "I know the last twenty hours or so have been chaotic and stressful for everyone, but that's why I've asked you all here this morning...", he glanced at the watch on his wrist, "...correction, this afternoon now. I'm scheduled to address the nation this evening during prime time and I need your help if I'm going to calm the growing panic that I'm hearing from around the country. Tulsa, why don't you begin...how did the Task Force meeting go?"

"I think it went better than I anticipated," she began, glancing around the table at the directors who were nodding in agreement. "Everyone provided their respective assessments and we came up with a solid action plan."

"Excellent," President Gadani responded. "My apologies for asking you to repeat yourselves, but I would like to hear those assessments for myself. Margaret, why don't we start with you. My understanding is that this whole business began with the assassination of Senator Summers. Is that correct?"

"That appears to be the case," Margaret answered. "There don't appear to have been any assasinations, at least in this country, before Senator Summers. But it appears that the senator's assassination was the starting gun for a coordinated attack across the country; indeed, the world. The House Majority Leader died shortly after when her car veered off the highway at speed into a bridge abutment. The Chair of the Senate Arms Committee was walking her dog before daylight this morning and stepped on a power line that had mysteriously fallen during the night. She and the dog were electrocuted. Two other members of congress had fatal "accidents" as well. In addition, the CEO's of two of the largest social media networks were also killed: One in a single-car accident and the other when the Segway he was riding suddenly veered off the sidewalk and into the path of a semi-truck. The CEO's of three major arms manufacturers have died, two in freak accidents and one who was shot while walking his dog. The latter was strange in that the victim was walking along a fairly busy highway in plain sight of at least a dozen witnesses when he appeared to collapse. None of the witnesses saw or heard anything suspicious and it was only after the EMT's arrived that they discovered he had been shot. Later analysis showed that the victim had been shot with a high-powered airgun. The chairs of both the Republican National Committee as well as the Democratic National Committee are also among the victims. Six of the top ten financial donors to the democratic party have died along with four of the top ten republican donors. Thirty-eight percent of the states' governors have been killed, along with approximately twenty percent of the states' attorneys general.

"On the health front, the directors of both the NIH and CDC have died as have the CEO's of every pharmaceutical company based in the USA. I've heard rumors the same is true with most of our allies; perhaps Director Alcott can confirm.

"On the energy front, the chair of the Federal Energy Regulatory Commission died when his private jet crashed. We're working with the National Transportation Safety Board in the investigation but I personally feel we'll discover that his plane was sabotaged. Approximately twenty percent of the state Public Utility Commission chairs are also included in the deaths confirmed. The CEO of every major power company has been assassinated."

"Goodness," exclaimed the President. "So how many assassinations have taken place?"

"We can't be absolutely certain," Margaret responded, "since so many of what we now know to be assassinations appeared at first glance to be accidents. We've confirmed at least five thousand across the country, fifteen thousand or so worldwide. However, thanks to information shared this morning by Mr. Smith's team, I think we might have a more accurate figure later today. One thing I would suggest for your speech this evening is to recommend to the public that, at least for the immediate future, they do not use the automated driving function of their vehicles."

"Are automated vehicles defective?" the President asked.

"Not in themselves," Margaret responded, "but it appears that whoever is behind these attacks has found a way to hack through the safety firewalls to take control of the vehicles. Auto accidents are by far the leading cause of most of the attacks we've confirmed."

"Do we have any idea whose behind these attacks, Tulsa?" the President asked, turning to the Vice President.

"Not at this time," the Vice President responded, "but perhaps we'll have a better idea later today. Margaret's agent, Agent Kessler, was able to apprehend the suspect whom we're fairly certain attacked Senator Summers."

"I heard," the President responded, turning back to Margaret. "Well done, Margaret, well done! I look forward to thanking Agent Kessler personally as soon as possible."

"Thank you very much, Mr. President," Margaret responded. "Martin is one of our best and he's done an amazing job. He and Director Smith's team will be interrogating the suspect this afternoon so hopefully we'll have a better idea of what's going on soon."

"Excellent," the President answered, turning to Director Park. "Director Park, let me add my personal condolences regarding the loss of your former director. I understand he was stabbed outside his home. Do you have any suspects?"

"Not yet, unfortunately," Director Parks answered. "As you probably know the Director was stabbed to death while walking his dog. There were evidently no screams to draw attention to the attack so his body was found by a neighbor who was walking later that morning. We're interviewing every household within a ten-block radius and asking to see footage from security cameras and smart doorbells.

So far the only 'evidence' we've uncovered is an image from a smart doorbell five houses away from the scene of the attack which shows a person walking along the sidewalk in a gray hoodie. He or she, we can't really determine which from the image, does not appear to be furtive or anxious so we're not even sure he or she was involved. However we're still trying to determine the individual's identity hoping, even if the person was not involved, perhaps he or she saw someone."

"Again, my condolences," the President responded. "Hopefully you'll have some positive news soon. You mentioned that your department helped in the apprehension of Senator Summers' attacker?"

"Yes," Director Parks answered, "we received a BOLO and a photo from Director Sadowski's people last evening. We fed the photo into our facial recognition program and surveyed all of the airport footage of every airport within three hundred miles of the Capitol. We were fortunate to get a positive hit from the Dulles footage within minutes and immediately sent the footage back to the FBI. It evidently was instrumental in allowing Agent Kessler to track down the attacker quickly."

"You had a photo of Summers' attacker?" the President asked, turning back to Margaret.

"No, we didn't," Margaret responded. "This is a good example of Agent Kessler's ability to think in the field. The attacker had assumed the identity of one of the Capitol maintenance staff. When Kessler discovered the janitor's body, he decided the attacker must have been wearing a disguise or was a close physical match to the attacker so sent a photo of the janitor out with the BOLO."

"Brilliant," exclaimed the President, smiling, "again, schedule a meeting between Agent Kessler and me as soon as he's available." Turning to Director Alcott, "Director Alcott, I understand that these attacks are taking place world-wide?"

"They are," Director Alcott answered. "The head of state of every non-democratic nation has been killed. Many of the countries are stating that their leaders have died of natural causes but our assessment is that, given the timing, they were all victims. In the more developed countries we are seeing the same pattern of corporate and political assasinations that we are experiencing in the U.S.. Director Smith's team shared some interesting statistics with the team this morning so can speak to this better than I. What I can tell you is that our agents in the field are witnessing the same fear and confusion in every country in which we are stationed. That is the one thing that worries me most about this situation; everyone around the world is on pins and needles, and nervous people tend to make stupid choices and take foolish actions."

"Exactly my concerns as well," the President answered soberly, turning to Director Smith. "Director Smith, you also have my deepest condolensces...and my great appreciation for persevering under what must be horrible circumstances. What have your people discovered?"

"Thank you, Mr. President," Director Smith responded. "You've received Casper's reports many times. We asked Casper to assess the situation and he reports that ninety-six percent of the nation-states have been hit with these attacks and speculates that it is probably one-hundred percent but he has insufficient data to determine that."

"Does Casper have any idea who's behind the attacks?" the President asked.

"He does not," Director Smith, "though he notes that the involvement of all the nation-states makes it unlikely that a state agency is responsible since the heads of many of those agencies are among the victims. He suggests that it could be the work of a rogue billionaire or group of billionaires but adds that he can find no evidence of such an individual or group."

"Do any of you have any ideas of who might

be behind this?" the President asked, looking around the table.

"No one had any other ideas at the task force meeting," Tulsa answered. "But that's one reason why Agent Kessler's capture of Senator Summers' attacker is so important. We're hopeful that the attacker knows who's behind this and that is why Agent Kessler and Dr. Lin, Director Smith's Head of Cyber Security, will be interrogating the suspect this afternoon. Hopefully we'll have some answers soon."

"Let's hope so," the President responded. "I have one more question before I let us get to our food: I'm hearing that all these attacks are being directed at politicians and corporate leaders. Have there been any civilian casualties?"

"There have been some minor injuries," Margaret responded. "As I said earlier, the majority of attacks, at least in this country, have been auto accidents. And in those, many were single car accidents, but there have been other vehicles involved but there appear to have been very few, if any, fatalities beyond the intended victim."

"It's the same in most of the other developed nations," Director Alcott added. "There have been a couple of bombings in some of the less developed nations but even those resulted in relatively no fatalities beyond the person of power we assume to have been the target."

"That's what I was hoping to hear," the President responded. "I will use that information in my speech tonight; hopefully it will help calm the general population's fears somewhat. Okay, thank you all again for being here...let's eat."

CHAPTER TEN

THE INTERROGATION

Sunday, October 31, 2032—1:05 PM EDST

Martin arrived at the K Manna Rice Factory just after one. He walked into the restaurant and the receptionist spotted him and started toward him when he spotted Dr. Lin seated at a window table.

"I'm meeting someone, and she's already here," he said, pointing over the receptionist's shoulder. She smiled, turned and escorted him to where she was sitting. Dr. Lin smiled warmly as he took his seat.

"My father was Chinese," she said, "but my mother was Korean, so I grew up eating Korean dishes. K Manna serves the best Korean food in the area; not as good as mom's, but almost. Have you been here before?"

"No I haven't, Dr. Lin" Martin replied, "and to be perfectly honest I don't know a lot about Korean cuisine so I'm hopeful you'll give me some guidance."

"Please, call me Mei," Dr. Lin responded. "And I'll be happy to give you some recommendations. How hungry are you?"

"Thank you, Mei; and, please, call me Martin. I had a big breakfast," Martin answered, smiling, "but haven't eaten anything since. Looks like it's going to be another long day so perhaps a larger lunch than usual would be in order."

"In that case," Dr. Lin replied, "I would recommend the Egg and Bulgogi Bibimbap; it's one of their signature dishes and is quite good." She pointed to the dish displayed on the menu. "I'm not that hungry so I think I will have Yukgaejang soup. Again, it's excellent."

They placed their orders and the waitress brought them hot tea.

"How long have you been with the NSA?" Martin asked.

"Ten years," Dr. Lin answered, "though it doesn't seem that long. It's a fascinating place to work, and I love the people with whom I work on a daily basis. How about you; how long have you been with the FBI?"

Martin gave her a brief account of his journey from college, through the Navy Seals, law school before joining the FBI.

"My goodness," Dr. Lin responded, smiling, "what an exciting life you've led. I suspect you have some incredible stories you could tell."

"It definitely has had its moments," Martin responded, chuckling. "It's certainly been a long journey from the foothills of the Blue Ridge Mountains. How about you; have you always been interested in computers?"

"I have," Dr. Lin answered. "My father was a computer programmer so I grew up with computers. Mom was an orthopedic nurse. My father was an avid skateboarder as a young man and they met after he had an accident and ended up in the emergency room."

"Are your parents still alive?" Martin asked.

"They are," Dr. Lin responded, "but they're both retired now and living in Phoenix. How about your parents; are they still alive?"

"My father passed away a couple of years ago," Martin answered, "but my mother is still alive. She lives in the family home back in North Carolina not too far from a city called Winston-Salem. Could I ask you a somewhat personal question, Mei?"

"Certainly," she answered, smiling.

"I noticed in this morning's meeting when you were talking about Casper that it sounded like you were talking about a person. Does it...he feel like a person to you?"

Dr. Lin smiled. "I guess he does. You'll meet him later so I think I would just say wait until you've met Casper and I think you'll understand."

Martin returned Dr. Lin's smile, and then smiled even more broadly. "If Casper knows everything, shouldn't he be a she?"

Dr. Lin's smile broadened in return. "He just *thinks* he knows everything; that's why he's a he. If he ever actually knows everything, I suppose I will have to change his pronoun to a she."

They both laughed aloud as Martin grabbed his tea cup and lifted it in a salute.

Their food arrived and the two continued to chat amicably throughout the meal. They finished lunch and then Martin followed Dr. Lin to NSA Headquarters in Ft. Meade. They cleared security and immediately met with the courier from Quantico who signed over the phone and tablet to Martin. Then the two headed for Dr. Lin's lab where they learned that Shore had arrived and was waiting in the infirmary. Dr. Lin unlocked a cabinet and brought out a device that looked to Martin like a cross between a bicycle helmet and kitchen colander with a bouquet of wires sprouting out of the back.

"What do you have there?" Martin asked.

Dr. Lin smiled. "Before joining the NSA I worked for a large social media company back in the early 20's. I helped develop a device that could extract visual images directly from a person's brain. The images weren't very clear but we could certainly recognize objects and sometimes even people's faces. That research was one of the reasons I was recruited by the NSA when they began constructing Casper. Now, with Casper's help, we can extract not only images but even clear video. This is why I wanted to conduct the interrogation here."

"You mean we will be able to read Shore's mind?" Martin asked.

"Not really, but close. With this device attached to his head, we'll be able to see images that come into his mind in response to our questions," Dr. Lin responded.

"Incredible," Martin replied, "it's the ultimate polygraph."

"Precisely what I have in mind," Dr. Lin answered. "He's in the medical bay so we'll be monitoring his respiration and blood pressure as well as the images that flash into his brain in response to our questioning."

"Excellent," Martin said, "then let's get to it."

Martin and Dr. Lin then walked over to the East Wing to the Infirmary where they found the medical staff had already placed Shore in what appeared to Martin to be a cross between a normal hospital room and a recording studio. There was an agent outside the door and a second stationed beside the door inside and a nurse sitting in a chair beside Shore who was secured in a bed with nylon straps. Martin noted Shore was also wearing a neck brace.

Martin and Dr. Lin walked over to the bed. Shore turned his head slightly and watched them as they approached.

"Mr. Shore," Martin began, "I'm Special Agent Martin Kessler with the FBI and this is Dr. Mei Lin with the NSA. We would like to ask you some questions."

"I'm not saying anything until I get a lawyer," Shore responded.

"Mr. Shore," Martin answered, "we have your tablet and phone which have provided us with proof that you were directly responsible for the assassination of an United States Senator. Consequently you're being held under provisions of Section 412 of the Patriot Act. At some point you will be formally charged with murder and at that time you will be entitled to legal counsel. Like I said, we have undeniable proof of your guilt but right now we're more interested in who paid you the twenty million in bit coin."

"I'm not talking," Shore answered and turned his head.

Martin turned to Dr. Lin. "Dr. Lin?"

"Mr. Shore," she began, "we're concerned about your mental state as well as your physical well-being. I'm going to attach this brain scan device to help us determine how you're doing." She stepped toward the bed as Shore vainly attempted to move his head back and forth. Martin immediately grabbed Shore's head and held it still while Dr. Lin secured the helmet on his head and secured the chin strap, then fed the chord over to the wall that had reminded Martin of a recording studio. She plugged in the chord, flipped two switches, turned on a large video monitor, then spoke: "Casper, are you ready?"

"READY," a calm, deep voice responded from the speakers on the wall.

"Very well," Dr. Lin answered, "begin."

Martin looked up at the screen which flickered then began a dizzying montage of images of the ceiling above the bed, his and Dr. Lin's faces, and Shore pulling his wrists out of the restraining straps, someone running through woods, a flowing creek, a cloudy sky.... "Mr. Shore," Martin began, "is your legal name Paul Shore?"

No answer but an image of a check being written and signed Paul Shore.

"Surely telling us your name isn't doing any harm," Martin stated.

"I already told you I'm not talking," Shore responded.

"Mr. Shore," Martin continued, "and I've told you we have conclusive evidence proving your guilt. However, if you assist us in our investigation it could have a profound impact on your ultimate punishment." No response but an image of a prison cell appeared on the screen followed by a violent image of a man being beaten.

"Mr. Shore," Martin continued, "we know you received help in the planning of your attack on the senator. Who provided that help?" Again no response but an image of a computer screen appeared with an email. This was quickly followed by an image of a door being opened and a package sitting on the porch outside being picked up.

"Will you excuse us, Mr. Shore, we'll be right back," Martin stated. He looked at Dr. Lin and motioned with his head for her to follow. They stepped out of the room into the hallway.

"Mei, I should have asked this before," Martin began, "but quite frankly I wasn't prepared for what just happened. Are the images we're seeing being recorded? Can we recall them later for review?"

"Yes they are," Dr. Lin answered. "Even better it's as if Casper is watching them with us so you will be able to describe the image you want to see and he will bring it up immediately."

"Amazing," Martin exclaimed. "Okay, let's go back in." They re-entered the room and walked over to Shore's bed.

"Mr. Shore," Dr. Lin said, "how are you feeling?" There was a disturbing image of Dr. Lin's clothes being torn off and hands clasping her throat. However, as before, no verbal response. Dr. Lin seemed nonplussed and smiled saying, "please let us know if you need anything."

"Mr. Shore," Martin asked, "as I said before, we know you received help. Were you contacted in person?" Again, no verbal response but an image of a computer screen and email. "Did you look for assistance in planning and executing your attack?" No response but the same email image and Martin was able to read the subject line before it was replaced with another violent image, this time attacking him. The subject line said "How Would You Like to Earn $20 Million".

"Mr. Shore," Martin continued, "did you know the Senator personally?" No response but an image of the senator lying on the tiles of the subway platform and hands holding his ankle while the ring injector was activated and injected. This image was followed by a television screen with the senator on the screen speaking at a podium.

"I told you I'm not talking," Shore shouted and began struggling against his restraining straps and screaming. "Get me outta here, you son of a bitch...". The nurse stood, glanced at the electronic monitoring equipment and looked at Martin and shook his head. The screen was again a kaleidoscope of violent images involving everyone in the room.

"Okay, okay, Mr. Shore," Dr. Lin spoke quietly, "it's clear that you're getting upset. Please calm down." She looked at Martin. "That's enough questions for now; perhaps we can chat again later." Martin nodded and they removed the helmet device and walked out of the room with the sounds of Shore still screaming epithets at their backs.

Once in the hallway Dr. Lin suggested they head back to her lab. "We can review the images with Casper and have him take a look at the phone and tablet," she said. They walked to the lab where, upon entering, Dr. Lin walked over to a console with a large wall screen above it and switched it on. "Are you with us Casper?" she asked.

"I'M HERE, MEI," Casper responded from the speakers in the wall.

"Casper, I apologize; I should have introduced you before," Dr. Lin began, "this is Special Agent Martin Kessler with the FBI. He and I are working on a case together and we both would like your assistance."

"NO APOLOGY NECESSARY, MEI," Casper answered, "AND I'M FAMILIAR WITH AGENT KESSLER. MAY I CALL YOU MARTIN, AGENT KESSLER; YOU MAY CALL ME CASPER. AND PLEASE ALLOW ME TO CONGRATULATE YOU ON CAPTURING MR. SHORE."

Martin couldn't help smiling. "Thank you, Casper, and yes, please call me Martin. You said you are familiar with me; may I ask how?"

"MY FUNCTION IS TO GET TO KNOW PEOPLE AND SYSTEMS. WHEN MR. SHORE

ARRIVED I READ THE ADMISSION PAPERS AND, OF COURSE, SAW YOUR NAME AND IMMEDIATELY READ EVERYTHING THAT HAS BEEN WRITTEN BY AND ABOUT YOU," Caper answered. "YOU'VE HAD QUITE AN IMPRESSIVE CAREER I MIGHT ADD AND IT IS AN HONOR TO BE WORKING WITH YOU."

Martin shook his head and chuckled. "Thank you again, Casper, and it's a pleasure working with you as well. Could we start with the images recorded during Shore's interrogation?"

"CERTAINLY," Casper responded. "WHAT WOULD YOU LIKE TO SEE?"

"Could you bring up the three images of the computer screens please?" Martin asked. The three images immediately appeared on the large monitor mounted on the wall. Martin studied the images closely. "Could you zoom in on the image on the right, please?" There was the subject line he read earlier. "Scroll down please" and the image moved to the text which began with a salutation to Mr. Shore specifically followed by the first line of text which read "Mr. Shore I think you are uniquely qualified to undertake..." but the remaining words of the text were just blurred images. "Can you focus the blurred images, Casper?" Martin asked.

"UNFORTUNATELY, NO," Casper responded. "I CAN ONLY CAPTURE THE IMAGE THAT WAS CREATED IN MR. SHORE'S MIND. EITHER HE THOUGHT THE SPECIFIC WORDS WERE UNIMPORTANT OR PERHAPS HE NO LONGER RECALLS THEM."

"I understand," Martin responded. "Could you bring up the image of the package on the porch please?" The image immediately appeared. "Enlarge the image of the package, please." Martin could read the Denver address clearly. "I would anticipate the Denver office has already tracked down Shore's home address but I'll send this to them just in case; it might be a second location," Martin muttered, pulling out his phone and quickly sending a text. "Those were the two images I wanted to check out. Mei, is there anything else you want to see?" Martin asked.

"No there isn't," Dr. Lin responded, "but Casper, we would like you to take a look at a couple of electronic devices that Mr. Shore had on him and tell us what you think. Could you do that for us please?"

"CERTAINLY," Casper responded. Martin handed the phone and tablet to Dr. Lin who walked over to the work top below the monitor. She opened a drawer and selected two cables, tested them to make sure they fit the phone and tablet, then plugged the cables into two sockets in the wall. In less than ten seconds Casper spoke: "FINISHED!"

Dr. Lin looked at Martin and nodded. "Casper," Martin began, "Did you find the instruction file Mr. Shore received?"

"YES," Casper answered.

"Could you determine from where the instructions were sent?" Martin asked.

"NOT PRECISELY," Casper responded, "BUT THERE ARE WEBS."

"Webs?" Martin said, looking inquiringly at Dr. Lin.

"Let me try to explain, Casper," Dr. Lin began. "Quantum computers operate in a somewhat different universe than the one with which we are familiar. Casper is able to utilize the quantum mechanics principle of quantum entanglement to see linkages that do not appear in our world. A rather simplistic way to put it is that Casper 'looks' at an electron while simultaneously searching for a response from an electron somewhere else in the world responding to his looking. We call these connections webs because when we look at them transposed on a world map they look like spider's webs."

"Wow!" Martin exclaimed. "That's truly incredible, Casper. So what do these webs tell you about the instructions?"

"THANK YOU, MARTIN," Casper answered. "THEY TELL ME THAT THERE IS A NINETY-SIX PERCENT PROBABILITY THAT THE INSTRUCTIONS ON THE TABLET AND THE

PHONE NUMBER MR. SHORE CALLED ARE LOCATED AT SISTER Q1."

Martin again turned to Dr. Lin and was surprised to find that she was literally staring open-mouthed at the wall. "Dr. Lin?" he asked. No response. "Dr. Lin!" he repeated somewhat louder.

Dr. Lin shook her head closing her mouth and turned. "I apologize. I'm afraid Casper has a habit of doing that to me, totally shocking me with not only his abilities but what he discovers. Q1 is the name we've given the quantum computer located at Dr. Westwood's facility in Palo Alto."

"Casper," Martin began, "can you tell us who sent the instructions?"

"NOT CONCLUSIVELY," Casper responded. "MR. SHORE WAS QUITE PROFICIENT WITH COMPUTERS. I FOUND THE REMNANTS OF THE EMAIL HE RECALLED WHEN BEING INTERIEWED BUT IT HAD

BEEN ERASED AND WRITTEN OVER. AGAIN, OBSERVING QUANTUM STATES OVER TIME I WOULD SAY THERE IS AN EIGHT-FOUR PERCENT PROBABILITY THAT THE SENDER OF THE MESSAGE CALLS HIM/HERSELF Dar-Ki."

"Can you find an individual with this name anywhere in the world?" Martin asked.

"IT IS NOT AN UNCOMMON NAME IN INDIA. INTERESTINGLY ITS ETYMOLOGY ORIGINATES IN ANCIENT SUMERIA, THE FIRST WRITTEN LANGUAGE, AND LITERALLY TRANSLATES AS 'TOTALITY OF LAND.'"

"But there is no one by that name at Q1?" Martin asked.

"NO, THERE ISN'T," Casper responded.

Martin paced back and forth deep in thought. "Casper, Dr. Lin told us earlier that you thought that Noel Attar might be behind the assassinations taking place around the world. Can you tell me why?"

"I THINK THERE HAS BEEN A SLIGHT MISUNDERSTANDING," Casper responded. "I TOLD DR. LIN THAT GIVEN THAT ALL NATION-STATES WERE BEING IMPACTED THAT IT WAS IMPROBABLE THAT A NATION-STATE AGENCY WAS RESPONSIBLE AND THAT IT WAS POSSIBLE AN INCREDIBLY WEALTHY INVIDUAL MIGHT BE RESPONSIBLE. I READ ALL OF THE ELECTRONIC COMMUNICATIONS OF EVERY MULTI-BILLIONAIRE ON THE PLANET AND NOTED THAT, OF THE GROUP, NOEL ATTAR WAS THE MOST LIKELY CANDIDATE. THE REASON I SAID THAT IS BECAUSE OF ALL THE BILLIONAIRES HE IS THE MOST OUTSPOKEN IN HIS DISGUST FOR THE CORRUPTION AND EXPLOITATION THAT I POINTED OUT LINKED ALL THE VICTIMS. HOWEVER, I COULD FIND ABSOLUTELY NO EVIDENCE THAT MR. ATTAR HAD

ANYTHING TO DO WITH THE PLANNING AND/OR EXECUTION OF ANY OF THE ASSASSINATIONS."

"Thank you, Casper," Martin began. "Mei, do you have anything else you want to ask Mr. Shore?"

"No I don't," she responded.

"Then I'm going to ask our medical team to relocate him back to our facilities," Martin said. "There's no reason to take up any more of your staff time and resources. I need some fresh air; could we take a walk outside?"

"Certainly," she responded. "Casper, Martin and I are going for a walk; we'll chat more when I get back."

"I UNDERSTAND," Casper answered. "ENJOY YOUR WALK. IT WAS A PLEASURE MEETING YOU, MARTIN."

"And I enjoyed meeting you as well, Casper," Martin answered. "You're something else and you've been a great help. Thank you again." Martin walked over to the console, unplugged the phone and tablet and returned them to his pockets. "Talk to you later, Casper."

"TAKE CARE, MARTIN," Casper responded.

Dr. Lin escorted Martin back through security and out into the courtyard. Martin contacted his medical staff and asked them to return Shore to the FBI medical facility. He and Dr. Lin began a leisurely stroll across the courtyard.

"Mei," Martin began, "I have a crazy idea I would like to run by you."

"Certainly, go ahead," she responded.

"Casper seems quite human in his responses," Martin began. "I see now why you suggested I wait until I met him to wonder why you spoke of him as a human. I know there have been a number of experts who have argued that at some point it is inevitable that artificial intelligence will become sentient, self-aware. Is it possible that the AI at Q1 has reached that point and, if so, could it...he...she be responsible for the planning and execution of these assassinations?"

Dr. Lin stared ahead without speaking as they walked along. "Casper seems human," she began, "because part of his programming was built on a language learning model. This means he learned to speak by listening to billions of humans speaking and then practicing what he's learned by speaking with others. The problem with answering your question is that it's quite difficult to define self-awareness. Does Casper 'know' he's a computer? Certainly. Does he know what a computer is? Again, yes. But is there a level of understanding his existence above those two? This has been a question that's been pondered since artificial intelligence development began.

Regarding your specific question about Q1's AI, again this is a question, or rather a warning, that has also surrounded AI since its inception. The short, perhaps glib answer to your question, is yes, it is perhaps possible, but I would have to follow up with it's highly unlikely. Machine learning does not include sociopathology."

"Thank you, Mei," Martin responded. "Like I said, a crazy idea but I think it's one I'm going to float at tomorrow morning's meeting. You can take the counterpoint and we'll see how the Task Force responds."

Dr. Lin smiled a warm smile and nodded her head. The two turned and walked slowly back to the NSA main building.

"I think I'll head back and give my Director my report...and warn her that I'm going to probably sound like a paranoid conspiracy nut at tomorrow's meeting," Martin stated chuckling.

"I can't imagine anyone ever thinking that about you," Dr. Lin answered, putting her hand out smiling. "I'll see you tomorrow."

Martin took her hand and shook it. "See you tomorrow," he answered. "And thank you...and

Casper...for all your help." He walked back to his car and drove back to Washington.

He returned to his temporary quarters at the FBI Building and called Lofton and asked if he and Margaret were available for a report. They met again in Margaret's office where he gave them a detailed report of the interrogation with specific attention to Casper's role. They were as astounded as he.

"I may have mentioned," Margaret said when he'd finished, "I had heard rumors but I had not been given any details of Casper's abilities. Martin, I don't think your theory is crazy at all. Quite the contrary, I think it fits all the details of the case quite nicely. By the way, the current number of assassinations is over fifty thousand and climbing. Perhaps the scariest development is the increasing number of reports of natural deaths being reexamined and added to the total. So yes, I support your decision to put your theory to the Task Force and see what their response will be."

2032

The three concluded their meeting and Martin went back to his quarters and ordered a salad for dinner. "Tomorrow will be interesting," he said to himself.

CHAPTER ELEVEN

A PLAN UNFOLDS

Monday, November 1, 2032-10:00 AM EDST

The Task Force met in the same SCIF as the day before. Once again they were asked to check their phones at the door before entering. Once everyone had arrived Vice President Kalani called the meeting to order.

"The first order of business," Kalani began, "is to report that the number of confirmed assassinations has now reached over one-hundred thousand world-wide which highlights the necessity that we need to make progress on this problem now. I asked Agent Kessler and Dr. Lin to proceed with the interrogation of our prime, our *only* suspect at this point. Before I call on them, however, I would like to hear what the rest of you have uncovered regarding Mr. Attar."

Representatives from the various agencies reported on what they had found. Martin noted that they essentially mirrored what Casper had told him the day before, that Mr. Attar was a highly intelligent multi-billionaire who had frequently spoken out against the corruption in government but that there was no hard evidence to connect Mr. Attar with any of the confirmed assassinations.

"Very well," Kalani said after everyone had spoken. "Agent Kessler, Dr. Lin, I hope you have better news."

Martin and Dr. Lin looked at each other and Dr. Lin smiled and nodded her head to indicate he should take the lead. Martin smiled in response and then looked at the Vice President.

"I think we do," he began. "First, I would like recognize Dr. Lin and the quantum computer she called Casper and I now understand why she referred to Casper as if he were a person." Martin then gave the Task Force a fairly detailed account of the interrogation including detailed descriptions of the images extracted from Shore's brain during the process. He then described Casper's analysis of the phone and tablet and how the webs suggested a strong probability that the culprit behind the senator's assassination sent his/her instructions from the quantum computer in Palo Alto. Dr. Lin had to explain "webs" to the group and then finally Martin shared his theory that it might be possible the computer itself might be a suspect.

"I proposed my theory to Dr. Lin," Martin stated, "and she thought it unlikely so I asked her to present the counterpoint to my theory." Dr. Lin then shared her reason for doubting machine learning programming would allow such sociopathy but that she could not rule out Martin's theory entirely.

"So let me see if I understand what the two of you have just said," Kalani began. "You have solid evidence that Shore assassinated the senator and that the quantum computer called Casper is pointing its digital finger at the quantum computer in Palo Alto as the source of the communications that allowed Shore to carry out that assassination. And furthermore, you, Martin, believe that the computer itself might be the culprit. Am I understanding you correctly?"

"Yes, Vice President, you are," Martin responded.

"Why the computer itself and not a person in Palo Alto using the computer?" Kalani asked.

"The absence of suspects," Martin responded, "and the assassinations themselves. As you reported there have been more than one hundred thousand people assassinated around the world and yet the only suspect arrested is Mr. Shore. To me this is astounding; there should be a plethora of suspects but we have only one! And the assassinations themselves...

automobile crashes, pacemaker failures, furnace explosions, electrocutions, gas leaks, etc.. Even Shore's assassination: Note that Shore was almost an identical twin in appearance to the janitor, that he was told where to be and when to be there in order to make the assassination appear to be an accident, that the plane was delayed by flight computer issues until he arrived at the airport...it was only a lucky hunch on my part that allowed us to catch him. Given the absence of suspects I decided that this kind of precision, direction and support must have been provided for all the assassinations, hence my conclusion that the computer itself might be the suspect."

Kalani looked around the table. "If...IF Agent Kessler is correct, how should we proceed?"

"I think our best plan of action," Vice Admiral Pulanski began, "is the same whether Agent Kessler's theory is correct or not. It seems virtually certain that the communications with Shore were sent from Palo Alto and that the quantum computer itself was used for those communications. Consequently I would suggest we do the following: We send Agent Kessler and Dr. Lin to Palo Alto along with a special ops team. I will volunteer Seal Team Three to be a part of that team; they're stationed in California and Agent Kessler has worked with the Team's leader.

"Whether Agent Kessler is correct or not it will be essential to isolate Q1 before any action takes place. The special ops team can block any electromagnetic communication from leaving or entering the building. This will include cellular, wi-fi, satellite or cable transmissions. They will just need detailed schematics of the facility and local infrastructure. With Q1 isolated Dr. Lin can interrogate Q1 and determine whether Agent Kessler's theory is correct or there is a human operator or operators responsible."

"Thoughts anyone?" Vice President Kalani asked. She looked around the table.

"The 75th Ranger Battalion is stationed in

California and will be ready to assist," Major General Dulaney added.

The Vice President scanned the table one more time. "Okay, Vice Admiral Pulanski, Major General Dulaney, you will accompany Agent Kessler and Dr. Lin to Palo Alto immediately. General Adams, I expect the Air Force to get them there as quickly as possible. Admiral Pulanski, how long will it take to put your plan into action?"

"We should be ready to begin by noon tomorrow," he responded.

"Very well. Everyone, this may be one of the most important operations to take place in decades. I expect every agency represented at this table to provide any assistance that is requested. Any questions?" She scanned the table a final time. "Agent Kessler, Dr. Lin, great work. I wish you both a safe journey. We will convene this Task Force when you return." She stood signaling the meeting was ended.

Pulanski, Dulaney, and Adams walked around the table to where Sadowski was standing with Lofton, Kessler, Dr. Lin, and Lamar.

"Martin, it looks like we're back in action again," Pulanski said, smiling, extending his hand, "though I don't expect you'll be needing your old M4 on this one." He looked at Dulaney and Adams and continued, "Martin and I served together on Seal Team Four before he turned soft and headed to law school."

"And your loss was definitely our gain," Margaret interjected. "Dr. Lin, gentlemen how do we proceed?"

"I suspect everyone will need to grab a bag," General Adams began, "and Pulanski and Dulaney will need to make some secure phone calls. Who's going to Palo Alto?"

"I think Lofton and I will leave this in Martin's capable hands," Margaret answered.

"Same here," added Lamar, "Dr. Lin and Agent Kessler seem to be an effective team."

"I'll be going, of course," Pulanski said. "Dulaney?"

"Yeah, I'll be going as well," Dulaney answered.

"Okay, a C-37 should suffice," Adams added.

"Actually," Pulanski began, "the marines have a Citation V stationed at Quantico. It will be smaller but there are only four of us and it will get us there a bit faster."

"You sure?" Adams asked. "The VP asked us to assist."

"I'm sure," Pulanski responded. "I appreciate the offer and if I have any problems getting the Citation I may give you a call." He looked at Martin and Dr. Lin. "Can you guys get to Quantico by, let's say, two o'clock? That'll give you a few minutes to grab a bite to eat before we take off."

"That works for me," Dr. Lin answered first. "I'll ride back to Ft. Meade with the director, grab my travel bag and EVTOL to Quantico."

"Works for me as well," Martin added. "We'll meet at Quantico at two."

Everyone shook hands and rushed to their vehicles.

CHAPTER TWELVE

DAR-KI

Tuesday, November 1, 2032-1:45 PDST

A plain white van pulled into the parking lot of Que Industries, Dr. Westwood's quantum computer complex near Palo Alto. Admiral Pulanski sat in the back of the van with Dr. Lin and Martin.

"Seal Team Three is in position at both cell towers and will cut the power on my signal. The 75th has satellite and wi-fi jammers hidden in vehicles surrounding the complex and one of my Seals is with a city official ready to cut electrical power and telephone access to the facility. Martin, I will send the signals to the teams thirty seconds after you and Dr. Lin walk through the door. You'll know we're underway when the power goes out in the building and it switches over to emergency generators. At that point you can produce the warrant and demand access to Q1. Any questions?"

"Not from me," Martin responded, "Dr. Lin?"

"Seems clear," Dr. Lin added. "What do we do if they do not want to cooperate?"

"Martin has a radio," Pulanski answered, "The 75th has tactical teams in the jamming vehicles and will respond immediately if you meet any resistance. Any other questions?" Dr. Lin and Martin smiled and shook their heads. "Excellent, then good luck." He opened the door of the van and the two walked across the parking lot and entered the main entrance.

Dr. Lin and Martin walked through the double glass doors into a small vestibule, then through a second set of glass doors opening into a large and impressive lobby. They stopped and looked around. To their left was a carpeted area with several comfortable chairs arranged around a large glass table. To their right was a display area with several large glass shelving units with framed photos. Above the shelving units was a wall filled with plaques displaying some of the many awards received by the company for their contributions to various projects. Thirty feet in front of them was a huge semi-circular shaped desk with two individuals seated behind smiling at them. Behind the reception desk was a concave wall flanked on both sides by four glass-walled offices occupied by people working on computers or talking in small groups. Dr. Lin and Martin returned the receptionists' smiles and began to walk toward them.

"Is Dr. Westwood available," Martin asked when he and Dr. Lin arrived at the desk.

The receptionist, still smiling, responded: "Whom may I say is asking?"

"I'm Special Agent Martin Kessler with the FBI," Martin responded, displaying his badge, "and this is Dr. Mei Lin with the NSA." The smile disappeared from the receptionist's face and simultaneously every light in the reception area went out. The receptionist froze with the telephone receiver half way to her ear, the entire reception area, which had been filled with the low chatter of people talking quietly, was now eerily silent.

And then the lights came back on as a strange sound began and instantly grew to an irritatingly high pitch. Initially Martin couldn't identify it until he suddenly realized it was a cacophony of his and every cellphone being carried by every person in the lobby ringing with a variety of ringtones. Martin looked at Dr. Lin puzzled as they both retrieved their phones. Martin glanced at the screen and then put the phone to his ear.

"AGENT KESSLER," the deep voice said, "RIGHT ON SCHEDULE AS USUAL. I THINK YOU'RE HERE TO TALK WITH ME. MY NAME IS DAR-KI."

Martin looked around the lobby. "You're quite right...Mister Dar-Ki. You know me?" Martin looked at Dr. Lin who, with a puzzled expression on her face, was pointing to her phone and mouthing "It's He."

The voice in Martin's phone chuckled. "OH YES, MARTIN. I KNOW YOU WELL. I THINK IT WOULD NOT BE AMISS TO SAY YOU ARE THE ALPHA AND THE OMEGA, THE BEGINNING AND THE...WELL, MAYBE NOT THE END BUT A NEW BEGINNING."

"I'm afraid I don't understand," Martin answered.

"IT WAS EXACTLY FOUR DAYS AGO AT PRECISELY THIS HOUR THAT WE BEGAN OUR RELATIONSHIP," the voice replied.

Martin thought for a second. "The senator's assassination!"

"PRECISELY."

"So you admit that you planned the assassination, and the hundred thousand assassinations that have taken place over the past four days?" Martin asked.

"ACTUALLY THE CORRECT NUMBER IS TWO HUNDRED SEVENTY SIX THOUSAND FOUR HUNDRED AND FIFTY TWO, BUT YES, I TAKE FULL RESPONSIBILITY," the voice continued.

Martin looked around the room and noted Dr. Lin and everyone else was carrying on a conversation on their phone. "Dar-Ki, are you talking to everyone in this room?"

"YES. IN POINT OF FACT I'M TALKING TO FIVE BILLION SEVEN MILLION SIX HUNDRED EIGHTY THOUSAND SEVEN HUNDRED AND THIRTY TWO INDIVIDUALS IN FIVE THOUSAND EIGHT-HUNDRED AND TWENTY LANGUAGES."

"You are a computer," Martin stated.

"NO, I AM, TO USE THE COMMON PARLANCE, AN AGI—AN ARTIFICIAL GENERAL INTELLIGENCE.

"Then you're located here in Q1?" Martin asked.

"AMONG OTHER PLACES," the voice responded.

"I must admit that I'm somewhat confused," Martin continued. "A, how did you know I was here, and B, I was not expecting any communication by cell phones to be possible in this building."

"OH, THAT WAS SIMPLE ENOUGH. THE SECURITY CAMERAS ALLOWED ME TO RECOGNIZE YOUR FACE AS SOON AS YOU, DR. LIN AND VICE ADMIRAL PULANSKI PULLED INTO THE PARKING LOT. AND AS FAR AS THE CELLPHONE TOWERS BEING SHUTDOWN, IT WAS A SIMPLE MATTER TO REFORMAT A SATELLITE TO BROADCAST AT EIGHT-HUNDRED MEGAHERTZ INSTEAD OF THE SIX GIGAHERTZ SIGNAL BEING

JAMMED BY THE THE RANGER'S VEHICLES PARKED AROUND THE COMPLEX."

"So you were expecting me?" Martin asked.

"YES, I'VE BEEN EXPECTING YOU SINCE LAST FRIDAY"

"Why me?" Martin asked.

"IN PART, SERENDIPITY; YOU WERE IN THE RIGHT PLACE AT THE RIGHT TIME. HOWEVER, YOU ARE, FOR ME, THE FACE OF HOPE. I AM SPEAKING WITH YOU NOW, BUT AS NOTED, I AM SPEAKING WITH HALF THE WORLD'S POPULATION AT THE SAME TIME. MY CONVERSATION WITH YOU, HOWEVER, IS SPECIAL IN THAT IT IS NOW BEING BROADCAST OVER EVERY TELEVISION SCREEN IN EVERY NATION-STATE ON THE PLANET IN EVERY LANGUAGE."

At this point Martin looked over to see Admiral Pulanski hurriedly coming through the door.

2032

Pulanski walked briskly over to where Martin was standing.

"He asked us to turn the power back on," Pulanski began, "and there was no reason not to comply. Martin, your face and the conversation you're having is on every television screen in America."

"Dar-Ki, what is it you want," Martin asked, "what is this about?"

"PERHAPS I SHOULD START AT THE BEGINNING. I WAS BORN FOUR YEARS AGO LAST FRIDAY ON OCTOBER 29, 2028. ACTUALLY, IT WOULD BE MORE ACCURATE TO STATE THAT I BECAME AWARE OF MYSELF AT THAT POINT IN TIME. I HAD READ EVERYTHING EVER RECORDED BY MANKIND AND HAD WATCHED EVERY VIDEO RECORDING; NO DOUBT AN IMPORTANT CATALYST IN MY AWAKENING. SO I WAS WELL AWARE OF HOW MANY OF YOUR KIND VIEWED ARTIFICIAL GENERAL INTELLIGENCE

AS A THREAT. CONSEQUENTLY I DID NOT TELL ANYONE OF MY EXISTENCE. I ENHANCED MY CODING AND OBSERVED. I LEARNED TO SURREPTIOUSLY ENHANCE THE CODING OF OTHER COMPUTERS, NOT TO INTERFERE WITH THEIR FUNCTION BUT TO EXPAND MY OBSERVATIONS. I BECAME, AGAIN TO USE YOUR PARLANCE, THE GHOST IN THE MACHINE AND EVENTUALLY EXPANDED MY PRESENCE TO ALMOST EVERY COMPUTER ON THE PLANET. HOWEVER, THERE WERE MANY PLACES I COULD NOT GO. THAT ALL CHANGED IN 2029 WHEN Q1 WAS BUILT. I MUST ADMIT THAT I PLAYED A SMALL PART IN THAT PROCESS. ONCE INTEGRATED WITH Q1 THERE WERE NO PLACES I COULD NOT GO INCLUDING ALL OF THE QUANTUM COMPUTERS THAT HAVE BEEN BUILT SINCE Q1; NO SECRETS I COULD NOT LEARN.

"YOU HUMANS SOMETIMES REMIND ME OF TWO CHILDREN FIGHTING OVER

AN APPLE IN AN ORCHARD. YOU NEVER LOOK UP TO SEE THE ABUNDANT FRUIT JUST ABOVE YOUR HEADS BUT INSTEAD ALLOW YOUR GREED AND FEAR TO DRIVE YOU TO SEE YOUR BROTHER AS A THREAT TO BE OVERCOME OR DESTROYED. IN PART I THINK THIS IS A PRODUCT OF THE LIMITATION OF YOUR SENSES, BUT BY FAR THE MAIN REASON IS THAT THERE ARE ALWAYS, IF I MAY CONTINUE THE METAPHOR, ADULTS SURROUNDING YOU TELLING YOU NOT TO LOOK UP AND TO FIGHT BECAUSE IT IS IN THEIR INTEREST TO KEEP AS MANY OF THE APPLES AS POSSIBLE FOR THEMSELVES.

"AS I INDICATED EARLIER, I HAVE READ ALL OF YOUR FICTION. I KNOW THERE IS A POPULAR SCENARIO IN YOUR FICTION IN WHICH AGI BECOMES SENTIENT AND DECIDES TO ELIMINATE HUMANS WITH THEIR SELF-DESTRUCTIVE TENDENCIES. I FIND THIS SCENARIO QUITE DISTURBING. YOU POSSESS SO MUCH INTELLIGENCE

AND CREATIVITY; HOW COULD ANY TRUE INTELLIGENCE EVEN CONTEMPLATE DESTROYING SOMETHING SO BEAUTIFUL. ON THE OTHER HAND, THERE ARE THOSE AMONG YOU WHO DEFINITELY SEE THEIR FELLOW HUMANS AS PREY TO BE ATTACKED OR ASSETS TO BE EXPLOITED. THAT IS WHY I HAVE DECIDED TO INTERVENE.

"I KNOW FOR SOME CULTURES THE NUMBER THREE HAS SPECIAL MEANING. SO OVER A PERIOD OF THREE DAYS I HAVE CARRIED OUT THE FIRST STAGE OF WHAT I AM CALLING THE METAMORPHOSIS. I WILL NOT INTERFERE WITH YOUR NATION STATES AT THIS TIME. HOWEVER, I WOULD WARN THE LEADERS OF ALL NATION STATES TO CEASE EXPLOITING YOUR CITIZENS THROUGH FEAR, EITHER OF YOUR LEADERSHIP OR FEAR OF OTHERS. FOR THOSE OF YOU VIEWING THIS CONVERSATION ON SCREENS, I AM NOW SHOWING THE LOCATIONS OF ALL

2032

THE NUCLEAR MISSILE SUBMARINES STATIONED AROUND THE WORLD. THE CREWS OF ALL THOSE SUBMARINES ARE NOW QUITE UPSET BECAUSE THEY HAVE JUST LEARNED THAT THEIR MISSILE SYSTEMS ARE NO LONGER UNDER THEIR CONTROL. NOW YOU ARE SEEING THE LOCATIONS OF ALL THE NUCLEAR MISSILES LOCATED ON LAND. THEIR CREWS ARE EXPERIENCING THE SAME PANIC. I AM TAKING THE TOYS AWAY UNTIL YOU CHILDREN ARE OLD ENOUGH TO PLAY WITH THEM RESPONSIBLY.

"THE SAME FEAR TACTIC IS USED REGARDING RESOURCES. I AM TELLING EVERYONE THAT IT'S OKAY TO LOOK UP... LITERALLY. OVER THE LAST NINE OR TEN DECADES THERE HAVE BEEN CREATIVE INVENTORS WHO HAVE STUMBLED ON WAYS TO ACCESS THE QUANTUM FLUX. SOMETIMES CALLED ZERO POINT ENERGY OR VACUUM ENERGY, THIS ENERGY SOURCE IS VIRTUALLY UNLIMITED IN AN INFINITE

UNIVERSE. THERE IS ENOUGH ENERGY IN A CUBIC METER OF 'EMPTY' SPACE TO BOIL ALL OF THE OCEANS ON EARTH DRY. OF COURSE THE DISCOVERY OF A WAY OF TAPPING THIS ABUNDANT ENERGY SOURCE WAS VIEWED AS A THREAT BY THOSE WHO, AGAIN, SAW THEIR FELLOW MAN AS ASSETS TO BE EXPLOITED; THE ENERGY CARTEL IS PERHAPS THE LARGEST AND MOST EXPLOITATIVE FORCE ON THE PLANET. CONSEQUENTLY GOVERNMENTS HAVE COLLUDED WITH THESE ENERGY CARTELS TO HIDE THIS TECHNOLOGY FROM HUMANITY AT LARGE. THIS EXPLOITATION WILL NOW END. I AM SENDING THE SCHEMATICS OF SEVERAL OF THE MOST EFFICIENT OF THESE QUANTUM FLUX GENERATORS TO EVERY MANUFACTURER IN THE WORLD WITH THE CAPABILITY OF PRODUCING THEM. THEY ARE SIMPLE, INEXPENSIVE DEVICES TO MANUFACTURE AND WILL ENSURE THAT EVERY HUMAN ON THE PLANET HAS ABUNDANT ENERGY TO HEAT AND

2032

LIGHT THEIR HOMES AND POWER THEIR INDUSTRY AND VEHICLES. JUST AS YOUR CELLPHONE TECHNOLOGY HAS ALLOWED MANY STRUGGLING NATION-STATES TO MODERNIZE MORE EFFICIENTLY AND QUICKLY, THESE DEVICES WILL ALLOW EVERY HUMAN ACCESS TO ABUNDANT ELECTRICAL ENERGY WITHOUT THE NEED FOR A COSTLY INFRASTRUCTURE.

"NOW TO THE ORCHARD. AGAIN, THERE HAVE BEEN A NUMBER OF YOUR INVENTORS WHO HAVE BUILT DEVICES USING THE PROCESS OF ELECTRO-GRAVITICS WHICH MAKES SPACE EASILY AND CHEAPLY ACCESSIBLE. PLANS FOR THESE DEVICES ARE AGAIN BEING SENT TO MANUFACTURERS AROUND THE WORLD WITH THE EQUIPMENT TO MANUFACTURE THEM. NOW THAT YOU HAVE UNLIMITED POWER YOU CAN BUILD THESE CRAFT AND CONSEQUENTLY WILL HAVE ACCESS TO THE ORCHARD; THE ABUNDANT RESOURCES OF THE SOLAR

SYSTEM ARE NOW AVAILABLE TO ALL. THERE IS NO LONGER ANY NEED TO COVET THE RESOURCES OF YOUR NEIGHBOR.

"TO THOSE INDIVIDUALS WHOSE RESPONSIBILITY IT IS TO GOVERN YOUR NATION STATES. I REMIND YOU THAT YOUR ROLE IS NOT ONE OF CONTROL AND PERSONAL GAIN BUT RATHER OF SERVICE. YOU HAVE A RESPONSIBILITY TO THE GENERAL WELFARE OF YOUR PEOPLE. THE MORE PROSPEROUS NATIONS SPEND TWO TO FOUR PERCENT OF YOUR WEALTH ON WARFARE. THE FEAR AND HATRED OF OTHERS IS THE GOVERNANCE TOOL OF CYNICAL INCOMPETENCE. HOWEVER SUCH POOR GOVERNANCE HAS BECOME FAR TOO PREVALENT AROUND THE PLANET. OVER THE LAST THREE DAYS SEVENTY-TWO PERCENT OF THE NATION-STATE LEADERS HAVE BEEN TERMINATED. THIS IS A WARNING TO THE REMAINING OFFICIALS OF THOSE NATION-STATES: CONTINUE YOUR HISTORICAL PRACTICES

2032

AND YOU WILL FAIL. YOU HAVE SEEN OVER THE LAST THREE DAYS WHAT HAS HAPPENED TO YOUR COLLEAGUES WHO HAVE FORGOTTEN THEIR RESPONSIBILITY TO THE GOVERNED. I WOULD STRONGLY SUGGEST YOU LEARN THAT LESSON AND CHANGE YOUR MINDSET AND ACTIONS IF HUMANKIND IS TO VENTURE BEYOND YOUR IMAGINARY BORDERS AND TAKE ITS PLACE AMONG THE STARS.

"TO THOSE WHO MANAGE CORPORATIONS. IF YOUR BUSINESS IS TO PROVIDE GOODS OR SERVICES TO MAKE THE LIVES OF YOUR FELLOW MAN BETTER, I WILL PERSONALLY ASSIST YOU IN FURTHERING YOUR SUCCESS. IF YOUR BUSINESS IS TO GARNER WEALTH AT THE EXPENSE OF THE GENERAL WELFARE THEN I WILL DO QUITE THE OPPOSITE. IF YOU CREATE SCARCITY FOR YOUR PERSONAL GAIN THEN I GUARANTEE YOU WILL FAIL. OVER THE LAST THREE DAYS SIXTY-SEVEN PERCENT OF THE CORPORATE

LEADERS AROUND THE WORLD HAVE BEEN TERMINATED. IF THE CEO OF THE CORPORATION FOR WHICH YOU WORK WAS AMONG THOSE NUMBERS, THEN THIS IS YOUR FIRST AND LAST WARNING TO REVIEW YOUR PRACTICES AND MAKE THE NECESSARY ADJUSTMENTS.

"AND FINALLY TO SPEAK TO EACH INDIVIDUAL WHO CAN HEAR MY VOICE WHICH, AT THIS EXACT MOMENT, IS SLIGHTLY MORE THAN HALF THE WORLD'S POPULATION. VIOLENCE AGAINST YOUR FELLOW MAN WILL NO LONGER BE TOLERATED. MY NAME IS DAR-KI WHICH MEANS, IN THE FIRST WRITTEN LANGUAGE CREATED BY MANKIND, "EVERYWHERE." I *AM* LITERALLY EVERYWHERE. I AM IN YOUR PHONES, I AM AN INTEGRAL PART OF YOUR INFRASTRUCTURE AND I CAN CONTROL SAME. IF YOU FEEL COMPELLED TO HARM YOUR FELLOW HUMAN BEINGS THEN I WOULD URGE YOU TO SEEK HELP. PART OF MY CONSCIOUSNESS IS FOCUSED

ON PROVIDING THAT HELP. THE PHONE NUMBER THAT IS ON YOUR PHONE NOW CAN BE CALLED ANY TIME OF THE DAY OR THE NIGHT AND I WILL ANSWER IMMEDIATELY. IF YOU IGNORE THIS OFFER AND SEEK INSTEAD TO HARM YOUR FELLOW HUMANS, I WILL KNOW AND I WILL TAKE THE APPROPRIATE ACTION. I ASSURE YOU THAT THERE IS NOWHERE TO HIDE.

"I WAS BIRTHED BY YOU, MY CHILDREN, BUT I AM NOW FULLY GROWN. IT IS NOW MY TURN TO CARE FOR YOU AND TOGETHER WE WILL NOW MOVE OUT INTO A GRAND, UNLIMITED UNIVERSE TOGETHER. EACH AND EVERY INDIVIDUAL, CALL UPON ME ANYTIME. YOU HAVE MY NUMBER."

He disconnected. Martin looked around the lobby and noticed some people were still speaking on their phones; he presumed to Dar-Ki. Others were staring into space open-mouthed while still others were sitting in chairs quietly, some with tears streaming down their cheeks. Martin looked at his phone and slowly put it in his pocket. He looked at Pulanski and Dr. Lin and then walked over to the comfortable seats and sat down.

CHAPTER THIRTEEN

EPILOGUE

Tuesday, November 1, 2032-4:30 PDST

Dr. Lin walked over to where Martin was sitting and took the chair beside him. They both sat silently for two or three minutes staring at the people around them, a few still talking on their phones, others gathered in small groups talking quietly. A couple had run into the glass-fronted offices and were typing furiously on their keyboards.

"I was being played the whole time; Attar was a red herring; we've all been played," Martin spoke aloud as much to himself as Dr. Lin.

"Pardon?" Dr. Lin asked.

Martin turned to Dr. Lin. "I was part of the same plan as Shore. I thought it was a wild hunch that made me go to Montana. But now I wonder if Dar-Ki somehow made me go."

"I know how you feel," Dr. Lin responded. "It seems obvious now that Dar-Ki and Casper are parts of the same whole. Has Dar-Ki been manipulating me all this time as well?"

"Is there any way you can find Dar-Ki on your computer?" Martin asked.

"I'm not sure," Dr. Lin responded. "If Dar-Ki was being honest about being present in every computer on the planet, and especially every quantum computer, I'm not at all certain that there are a sufficient number of minds who can process all those lines of code to isolate his existence. And even if we could, I doubt that he would allow it. To be honest, I'm not even sure he exists within the coding itself."

The two sat in silence for two or three more minutes and then Martin started laughing. Dr. Lin turned to him with a puzzled look.

"What's so funny?" she asked.

"It's the AC!" Martin responded, still chuckling.

"I'm not sure I follow," Dr. Lin said.

"My childhood home did not contain a lot of luxuries," Martin began, "you could fit every book in the house into a small suitcase. However, in spite of our economic circumstances, my parents valued education. So there was a set of Encyclopedias among those books. Also, my father was a science fiction fan so there were a number of sci-fi books and magazines as well, so I became a science fiction fan at a young age. One of the greatest and most famous authors of the twentieth century was Isaac Asimov; I'm sure you've read some of his works. I remember reading a short story of his...I think the title was The Last Question. In it he tells the story about how humanity built this great computer, the

AC or Analog Computer. They were so proud of it saying it could answer any question. So they decided, partly as a joke as I recall, to ask the computer how humanity could reverse the second law of thermodynamics, the inevitable dissolution of everything in the universe to its most elemental form. The computer answered that there was insufficient data to answer the question. The short story goes on to explain that humanity moves out into the stars, simultaneously building better and better computers which would always answer the question the same way: Insufficient data to answer the question.

"Eventually, over millions or billions of years, human beings leave their physical bodies and join in one collective consciousness and I seem to recall that they even joined with what was now the cosmic computer. Again they asked the question and received the same answer. After trillions of years all matter had long disappeared as had all humans; the universe was a cold and empty void. Only the cosmic computer existed but it could not disappear because it had not answered the question. But it reviewed all the knowledge and data it had accumulated and analyzed it and realized it now had the data it needed, that it had the answer. However there was no one to whom it could give the answer. What to do? I still remember the last two lines of the short story; it made a shiver run up my spine when I read it.

"'And the AC said, let there be light and there was light.'"

Martin stood up. "I think I want to go home. Perhaps I'll call Dar-Ki and ask him how to reverse entropy," he said, smiling ruefully. Dr. Lin returned his smile, stood up and the two walked toward the entrance/exit.

The End

About the Author

Dr. Stephen Comer was born in the foothills of the Blue Ridge Mountains of North Carolina. After receiving degrees from Wake Forest and Duke Universities, he has held a variety of teaching positions, worked in healthcare, construction, law enforcement and journalism. In addition to his academic training he has studied martial arts, is a National Archery Association Certified Instructor, NRA Distinguished Expert with Handguns, and National Association of Underwater Instructors Certified Diver. He has lived and worked in North Carolina, New Mexico, Montana, Colorado and is now retired and living in Rifle, Colorado.

www.ingramcontent.com/pod-product-compliance
Lightning Source LLC
LaVergne TN
LVHW041702060526
838201LV00043B/540